SHERLOCK HOLMES
MYSTERY MAGAZINE

VOL. 6, NO. 3   Issue #18

Publisher: John Betancourt
Editor: Marvin Kaye
Non-fiction Editor: Carla Coupe
Assistant Editor: Steve Coupe

Sherlock Holmes Mystery Magazine is published by Wildside Press, LLC. Single copies: $10.00 + $3.00 postage. U.S. subscriptions: $59.95 (postage paid) for the next 6 issues in the U.S.A., from: Wildside Press LLC, Subscription Dept. 9710 Traville Gateway Dr., #234; Rockville MD 20850. International subscriptions: see our web site at www.wildsidemagazines.com. Available as an ebook through all major ebook etailers, or our web site, www.wildsidemagazines.com.

FROM WATSON'S NOTEBOOK

Mrs Hudson is engaged in a long-delayed and much-deserved vacation, but she will be returning to 221 Baker Street at the beginning of next month and will, she told me in a recent letter, have a new column for SHMM # 19; she says that she has already written it—and asks to remind our readers to write her for advice or any other appropriate matter.

My recounting of the problem of the "Copper Beeches" may be found below. Also, appropriately, "The Adventure of the Copper Breechloads," in which Zakariah Johnson, working from my notes, tells of the time when Holmes and I met the famous American sharpshooter Annie Oakley.

I was quite intrigued by Janice Law's story of "The Holmes Impersonator." I tried to get Holmes to read it, but as I expected, its title put him off. Ah, well!

—John H Watson, M D

⚔ ⚔ ⚔ ⚔

For the first time in this issue of *Sherlock Holmes Mystery Magazine,* I have elected to run an article serially. "A Breton Homecoming" by Peter James Quirk, who has appeared here before, is a fascinating personal history of incidents during World War II, but its length has necessitated my asking him to divide it into two installments.

A second article by Lisa Cottagio speculates on the virtues and differences of books and screenplays.

New stories by Steve Liskow and Laird Long appear below, as does a short, personal reminiscence by my friend and colleague Carole Buggé. A rather creepy tale, "Spiders," was written by the pseudonymous Cenydd Ros, and a borderline fantasy told by a many-times murderer is the work of Steven Shrott.

Next issue will offer new stories by repeat authors Janice Law, Steve Liskow, Laird Long, J. P. Seewald, and Roberta Rogow, as well as other tales.

AND the following SHMM, number 20, will be devoted entirely to Sherlock Holmes.

Canonically Yours,
Marvin Kaye

COMING NEXT TIME...

STORIES! ARTICLES!
SHERLOCK HOLMES & DR. WATSON!

*Sherlock Holmes Mystery Magazine #19
is just a few months away...watch for it!*

Not a subscriber yet?
Send $59.95 for 6 issues (postage paid in the U.S.) to:

**Wildside Press LLC
Attn: Subscription Dept.
9710 Traville Gateway Dr. #234
Rockville MD 20850**

You can also subscribe online at
www.wildsidemagazines.com

ASK MRS HUDSON

by (Mrs) Martha Hudson

Dear Mrs H:

As I am a chef from India and pride myself on the fiery curries that I make in a restaurant in Soho, I wonder whether your tenants Mr Holmes and Dr Watson care to dine on such spicy cuisine?

Amaramus Kasaytana

Dear Mr Kasaytana,

Indeed, they do! Dr Watson acquired a taste for such food when he was in the army, and Mr Holmes says that he enjoys both Indian and Szechuan dishes because they are "refreshingly unlike the bland fare for which England is famous, or perhaps I should say infamous."

You will find below a chicken curry recipe that I have served them to much praise, though it may perhaps seem rather mild to you. Also, I believe that it is more usual to make curry with lamb or beef. If you would be so kind as to send me one of your own recipes, I will happily prepare it for my gentlemen guests. (By the way, I must say that even my curry is too much for my palate, which I confess is comparatively bland.)

Mrs Hudson

✗　✗　✗　✗

Dear Mrs Hudson,

Though I suspect I know the answer to the following question, I am quite curious concerning Mr Holmes's opinion concerning the existence—or not—of ghosts. I am, you see, a professional psychic healer trained in the tradition called by the Japanese "reiki". I have had numerous ghostly encounters, most of them in Edinburgh.

Professor Robert F Monrovia

My Dear Professor Monrovia,

I am sure that the answer you anticipate is that Mr Holmes has no interest whatsoever in this subject, regarding it as—in his words —"utter twaddle," a view shared by his elder brother Mycroft.

However, I think there may be something in it, after all, and that is partly because Dr Watson keeps an open mind on the subject, and probably because his literary agent, a Scottish gentleman named Arthur Conan Doyle, is a devoted spiritualist.

Regarding your experiences in Edinburgh, the coeditor of this magazine, Mr Kaye, completely agrees with you. He told me, "I lived for a few months in Scotland's capital and had several ghostly encounters myself, though I never saw them, but the feelings I had were quite powerful and upsetting. And when I inquired about the history of the places where I felt these 'vibes,' I always found out that they had ominous histories. As for believing in ghosts, I cite the late psychic investigator Drew Beltane, who would counter the question with one of his own—'Do you honestly believe in Grand Central Station?'"

Mrs Hudson

✗   ✗   ✗   ✗

My Good Mrs Hudson,

Perhaps I should be writing this directly to Mr Holmes, but as I am thoroughly impecunious, I hesitate to intrude on such a famous gentleman when I fear I could not reimburse him for his time. But I am quite troubled, you see, because recently my husband of several years succumbed to some mysterious ailment that our physician was unable to explain away. Perhaps Dr Watson, at least, might do better with solving my problem. Leonard, my husband, suddenly was in great pain; there were red circles under his eyes and—

(Here my correspondent detailed the other symptoms, which I will spare my readers from wading through, as they are both detailed and upsetting.)

—so, Mrs Hudson, that is the sum of what happened. I am deeply suspicious; a man who has tried repeatedly to seduce me to his will has lately taken to becoming friends with my (now late) husband. This man is a pharmacist in my neighbourhood. His name is Sebastian Carter, and he is about fifty and has very poor eyesight. I do not know if these details are significant or not.

In distress,

(Mrs) Leonard Bolton

My Dear Mrs Bolton,

I have spoken with both Mr Holmes and Dr Watson, and assure you that neither of them would even think of charging you for their assistance, which has been already rendered. And now, here is Mr Holmes's solution to your problem:

Dear Lady,

You are indeed correct. Your husband was foully murdered. I have despatched Scotland Yard to apprehend this villainous pharmacist. As to the method employed, it took considerable effort on Watson's and my part, but the fact that he is a pharmacist with eye trouble led us to explore the many medications and related substances that he has access to, and finally we visited his shop and obtained his own advice for dealing with the optical problem that he has.

Thus we determined that the most deceptively simple and seemingly innocent substance imaginable... *eye drops!!!*... are capable of poisoning with severe pain.

I venture to assume that under the guise of his alleged friendship with your husband, the scoundrel put these eye drops in a glass of whisky.

Yours in Sympathy,
Sherlock Holmes

⚔ ⚔ ⚔ ⚔

As promised, here is my curry recipe, as well as two others:

CURRIED CHICKEN

1 5-pound chicken, cut into pieces
1 clove garlic, chopped
2 onions, chopped
½ cup of oil
2 tomatoes, chopped
1 teaspoon salt
1 tablespoon curry powder
½ teaspoon ground pepper
1 teaspoon cumin
1 teaspoon coriander
¼ teaspoon cinnamon
2 bay leaves
3 cardamom seeds

1 teaspoon paprika
2 bay leaves
3 whole cloves
Indian Pale Ale (optional)

1. Fry garlic and onions in the oil.

2. Add the tomatoes and heat for five minutes.

3. Blend salt, pepper, curry powder, cumin, coriander, cinammon, cloves, cardamom, paprika, and bay leaves.

4. Add the blended spices to the tomato-garlic-onion mixture and heat for ten minutes.

5. Add the chicken and cook it till it becomes brownish, flipping it a few times.

6. Once the bird has turned brown, add the India Pale Ale, if desired, then cover the pot and place it in the oven.

7. Bake it for an hour at 325 degrees, basting it frequently.

8. Serve over rice.

✗　✗　✗　✗

The following is a pleasant dish that is one of Mr Holmes's favourite vegetable concoctions, for he remembers eating it whenever one of his French relatives came to visit his father.

SQUASH AND CHEESE PLATE

5 pounds of zucchini and yellow squash, sliced into ½ inch strips.
4 big onions, sliced thin.
6 ounces of gruyere cheese, grated.
1 cup of ricotta cheese.
2 big cloves of garlic, diced.
1+ ½ teaspoon of salt.
Ground pepper.

1. Place zucchini and squash in a big pot and cover with water.

2. Boil for 30 minutes, or until the vegetables have become tender.

3. Add the vegetables and seasonings and stir well.

4. Taste, and if necessary, fix it as desired.

5. Butter a large casserole dish and transfer the mixture to it. Cover with plastic and refrigerate.

6. When dinner is nearly ready to be served, heat the oven to 400 degrees.

7. Uncover the casserole and bake it for approximately half-an-hour or until it becomes bubbly and turns golden brown.

✗ ✗ ✗ ✗

Now let us conclude with that oh-so-traditionally British dessert known as trifle. It is, of course, really not cooked, but rather assembled. There is no one way to prepare it; every cook/chef has her or his own method(s) of preparation.

MRS HUDSON'S TRIFLE

½ dozen lady fingers.
1 packet of gelatin, any flavour.
A quantity of fruit, nearly any kind, but not fresh: canned or frozen. (Personally, I use fruit cocktail.)
Sherry wine, if desired.
1 packet of pudding or pie filling.
Whipped cream, if desired.

1. Place the lady fingers in the bottom of a fair-sized bowl.

2. Make the gelatin and pour it on top of the lady fingers.

3. Wait for the gelatin to become firm.

4. Place the fruit on the top.

5. Pour the sherry, if desired, over the fruit.

6. Prepare the pudding or pie filling (one could use both).

7. Wait for the pudding/filling to firm itself.

8. Place it above the fruit.

9. Cover with whipped cream, as desired.

SCREEN OF THE CRIME

by Kim Newman

Considering that Arthur Conan Doyle specifies that Sherlock Holmes's family comes from Yorkshire, it's a quirk that everyone—with the exception of Peter Cook—who has ever played the role adopts the incisive clipped accent thought of as BBC English. It's always struck me that a Holmes ought to sound like Sir Ian McKellen, whose natural Leeds accent is discernible in his normal speaking voice, but modified by Shakespearean training in most of his performances. Cast in *Mr Holmes*, William Condon's film version of Mitch Cullin's novel *A Slight Trick of the Mind*, McKellen finally gets to play the role, though this Holmes is a shadow version of the Great Detective, haunted by versions of himself—all of which are less real, but seem more authentic.

On a visit to Japan in 1946, where he pokes around in the ruins of Hiroshima for a miracle herb to combat the beginnings of the Alzheimer's which is erasing his personality, he disappoints his host's mother when—in a melancholy paraphrase of Billy Wilder's witty *The Private Life of Sherlock Holmes*—he sadly admits he didn't bring the deerstalker or the pipe of his popular image because they were added by the illustrators of his friend John Watson's fictionalised accounts of his adventures. Later, peeling back another layer of reality, he admits that he did once smoke a pipe, but stopped because he felt ridiculous when he looked like himself after Watson, Sidney Paget and the public created and accepted a heroic version of Sherlock Holmes.

Later, McKellen, in Dick Smith circa *Little Big Man* quality old age make-up by Dave Elsey, sits in a matinee audience to watch *The Lady in Grey*, a plausible 1947 film of a fictional fiction (Watson's 'The Case of the Dove Grey Glove'), in which a black and white Holmes is played by a grown-up Nicholas Rowe, erstwhile star of Barry Levinson's *Young Sherlock Holmes*. This is a tidied version of what is later revealed to be Holmes's final case, the failure which prompted him to retire to Sussex to keep bees. The reteaming of Condon and McKellen in another story about an elderly genius and a conflicted protégé evokes their work on *Gods and Monsters*, whereas a moment in which the ancient Holmes contorts himself to assume the pose of the girl in Andrew Wyeth's painting *Christina's World* echoes Terry Gilliam's film of Cullin's *Tideland*, which is to *Alice in Wonderland* what *Mr Holmes* is to Arthur Conan Doyle's Holmes canon. There are several mysteries to be solved—though Holmes's only real success is in pinning the mass-stinging of his protégé Roger Munro (Milo Parker) on some wasps to exonerate his bees—but the thrust of the story is to question solutions that don't help anyone.

Young Roger scorns his mother (Laura Linney) for barely being able to read, while delighting in the puzzles of Holmes's cases and his apiary pursuits, though Mrs Munro quite sees the dangers of such aspirations in that her mechanic husband sought to be promoted out of the motor pool only to be killed in action as part of a bomber crew. In the flashbacks, Holmes sees through the contradictory scheming of his client Mrs Kelmot (Hattie Morahan, who played Doyle's second wife Jean Leckie in the recent miniseries *Arthur and George*), a mystery full of Doylean clues and deductions, but solving the puzzle doesn't forestall a tragic outcome. *Gods and Monsters* also hinged on a murder-cum-suicide plot and an ageing genius, the director James Whale, struggling with the loss of faculties and using his undimmed skills to bring down the curtain on his achievements in style.

McKellen's Holmes, repressed where Whale was open, is another awards-worthy performance… though in representing a frail and fragile human character, he isn't really playing Sherlock Holmes except when he puts it on (when Roger insists he 'do the thing' and rattle off deductions) or makes it up (as in the final dramatised solution of the long-simmering Umezaki case). Like almost all films made in Britain, *Mr Holmes* benefits from casting in depth—here there's a perfect micro-cameo from John Sessions (who played Doyle in *Mr Selfridge*) as Mycroft Holmes, a melodramatic turn from Frances de la Tour as a sinister character (with Frances Barber brilliantly cast as her more glamorous movie incarnation), a briefly-glimpsed Colin Starkey as Watson, clipped representation of Scotland Yard from Philip Davis (the murdering cabbie in the first episode of *Sherlock*, 'A Study in Pink') and a brisk matter-of-fact turn from Roger Allam as a doctor who takes an un-Watsonian line in sternly offering the aged Holmes sound medical advice.

There has been a debunking tendency in Holmes films and fiction since Billy Wilder, from the psychological reductionism of Nicholas Meyer's *The Seven-per-cent Solution* to the depiction of the great detective as a 'high-functioning sociopath' or Chaplinesque scruff in recent TV and film versions, but *Mr Holmes* plays a subtler, more affecting game while retaining affection for Doyle's characters and their depths—note the perfect wordless reaction of a tea-bearing Mrs Hudson (Sarah Crowden) as she overhears her employer blithely assuring Mr Kelmot (Patrick Kennedy) that his wife's miscarriages oughtn't to have upset her too much.

✗　✗　✗　✗

BEES SAAL BAAD (1962)

Though it omits credit for Arthur Conan Doyle, this Bollywood box office hit is a fairly close adaptation of *The Hound of the Baskervilles* with the setting shifted from Dartmoor to Chandangarh in rural India (complete with a sucking swamp) and an apparent female ghost subbing for the Hound of Hell (as was the case in the 1909 Danish adaptation *Den Graa Dame*). All the familiar characters are represented: Dr Watson is a pith-helmeted moustached amateur detective bumbler Gopichand Jasoon (Asit Sen), Sir Henry is handsome aristocratic hero Kumar Singh (Biswajeet), Holmes is official Detective Mohan Tripathi (Sajjan), the Stapletons are heroine Radha (Waheeda Rehman) and her doctor father Ramlal (Manmohan Krishna), and Dr Mortimer and Barrymore the butler become Dr Pande (Madan Puri) and Laxman (Dev Kishan). In the prologue, an aristocrat rapes a girl who kills herself—and it's her ghost rather than the Hound which gets revenge by killing the dastard... and is supposedly responsible for wiping out most of the Singh family. The young heir returned from abroad hires private eye Gopichand to investigate the deaths in his family. The Holmes equivalent spends most of the film lurking suspiciously as he hops about on crutches, pretending to be a rural eccentric before a big reveal which comes when Gopichand accuses *him* of being the killer, only for the stalwart to throw away his crutches and accept the salutes of his fellow policemen.

Like many Bollywood films, it has to fit into several genres to provide a full evening's entertainment, so at least as much time is spent on the extended flirtation, romance and complications between Kumar and the villain's daughter as on the mystery and horror business. All the musical numbers belong to the love story side of the film and the plot has to stop sometimes to get comedy bits in from the bluff and blundering Gopichand. Director Biren Nag had obviously seen the 1958 Hammer Films version of *Hound of the Baskervilles*, since the scene in which Gopichand steps in quicksand and is hauled out by Ramlal is virtually identical to Terence Fisher's staging of the same sequence.

For any long-time Holmes fan, there's the repeated thrill of the familiar in a strange context: the flashback pursuit and abuse of the innocent girl, the lamp waved from the palace to alert the fugitive on the moor, the local doctor's suspicious involvement in the succession at the manor, the detective pretending to leave by train to use the hero as bait to trap the killer. Nag is at his best in the few horror movie moments—the initial stalking of the uncle by the long-nailed killer, the final unmasking of the furious Ramlal as the fake ghost and sundry skulkings in gloomy locales. In 1988, Rajkumar Kohli directed a very loose remake which drops almost all of the Holmesian overtones and deals instead with a family haunted by the ghost of a wronged woman.

✗   ✗   ✗   ✗

THE HOUND OF THE BASKERVILLES (1921)

Eille Norwood has the distinction of being the only one of a multitude of silent screen Sherlocks to own the role in the manner of Rathbone, Brett or Cumberbatch—eclipsing other contemporary portrayals and becoming the default Holmes for a generation. William Gillette and John Barrymore were bigger stars, but one was recreating his stage hit and the other crammed a Sherlock into a much more complicated screen career—and both drew on Gillette's play, which should really be seen as the first Holmes pastiche or fan fiction, rather than the original stories. Norwood and his preferred Watson (Hubert Willis) appeared in three series of short films based on the stories and Norwood starred in two feature films based on *The Hound of the Baskervilles* (with the grey, dignified, unmoustached Willis) and *The Sign of the Four* (with the younger Arthur Cullin stepping in to do the romance). Norwood got the Doyle seal of approval and his performance is sincere, focused and respectful—plus he has the proper beaky nose and casts a striking silhouette, whether seen from a distance on the moors (played by the real Dartmoor, which has rarely been done) or in shadow over a shot of a witness telling his story (one of director Maurice Elvey's striking touches).

As with all Holmes films until 1939, the assumption is that the story takes place in the present—with a motorised bus trundling out to Baskerville Hall and Beryl (Catina Campbell) in bobbed hair and a beret among so many tweedy or stiff-collared men. The story is slimmed down but played straight, which means that Norwood is offscreen for a long stretch while Watson is supposedly handling the sleuthing—indeed, Watson gets to shoot the dog here, while Holmes is off having a fistfight with Stapleton (Lewis Gilbert) in the mire. It seems screenwriters William J. Elliott and Dorothy Westlake took it that everyone read the twenty-year-old novel and don't bother much with concealing the villain's identity—he's seen in a false beard spying on 221 Baker St as Dr Mortimer (Allan Jeayes) and Sir Henry (Rex McDougall) consult Holmes and his lookalike portrait as wicked Sir Hugo is prominently displayed. Most screen Stapletons are exaggeratedly decent chaps in their early scenes, a tip-off as to their ultimate guilt, but Gilbert plays him like a glowering brute of the sort often seen in films of this vintage—it's not his scheming for the inheritance that makes us hate him, but that he beats up, knocks down and ties up his 'sister' (actually wife).

Beryl is given Pearl White-style escaping to do—burning the bonds with a knocked-over candle, tying the sheets into a rope. Barrymore (Fred Raynham), the butler, skulks in sinister fashion and signals to the doomed convict, who is his brother rather than brother-in-law here, but takes part in the rescue of Sir Henry from the dog, which is given an optical glow which comes and goes in the print I saw. In contrast with Rathbone, who celebrates the solution of the case by demanding 'the needle,' Norwood signs off by asking for a 'whiskey and soda.' It's too swift to be as atmospheric as it might be—the Dartmoor locations, augmented by a prop monolith, could have done with more exploring—but it does rattle along, proving this one of the most indestructible of all stories. Mme d'Esterre, the official Mrs Hudson of the series, appears briefly.

⚔ ⚔ ⚔ ⚔

TOM AND JERRY MEET SHERLOCK HOLMES (2010)

It's jarring that this starts with a Warner Brothers logo since it's a showcase for the MGM staple of cartoon characters. Joining Hanna and Barbera's Tom and Jerry (plus Spike and son from the later T&J cartoons) are Tex Avery's showgirl Red (once Red Riding Hood) and her beau the Wolf and hangdog hound Droopy and nemesis Butch. Indeed, the film finds room for fan-pleasing cameos for forgotten Avery one-offs like Simon LeGreedy from *Uncle Tom's Cabaña* (1947), the pilgrim from *Jerky Turkey* (1945), and the Kennel Master from *Out-Foxed* (1949). All this plus Arthur Conan Doyle's Holmes gang and a Victorian setting mixing humans and talking (or at least sapient) animals which evokes *Basil of Baker Street*.

The Warners Looney Tunes—Bugs, Daffy, Porky, etc.—existed in a shared world and were given to team-ups and feuds which extend to their feature outings in *Space Jam* and *Looney Tunes Back in Action*, but MGM didn't go that route, so it feels jarring that the very different cartoon universes of Hanna-Barbera and Tex Avery are lumped together, especially since it means two dim bulldog antagonists (Butch and Spike). The basic joke of Tom and Jerry was their never-ending unequal battle, where the seemingly superior cat would always be bested by the mouse (the secret of the series is that over time we came to hate the smug Jerry just as much as Tom does). The longstanding enmity is sidelined here as Tom and Jerry have to team up and work for the heroic Holmes (voiced by

Michael York) and Watson (John Rhys-Davies) in saving music hall star Red (Grey DeLisle) from blackmail which (with a nod to 'The Red Headed League') is designed to get her out of the house so 'the Star of Punjab' can be stolen by three cats with mechanical wings who work for Professor Moriarty (Malcolm McDowell).

Because they don't speak, Tom and Jerry aren't as versatile as some of their co-stars, so their main joke is malleable invulnerability as they are repeatedly squashed into odd shapes and pop back to their proper forms in a manner which makes them the animal equivalent of comic book types like Plastic Man or Mr Fantastic. The Earl Kress script has a lot of sweet Sherlockian in-jokes, like a Bruce Nigel Music Hall and a suspect called Brett Jeremy and a climax on a half-built Tower Bridge evokes the Guy Ritchie film. A few things have to be changed: this 221B Baker Street isn't a cluttered mess, because otherwise it wouldn't be funny when things get knocked over in slapstick chases.

Moriarty's scheme involves using stolen gems to create an eclipse-powered laser to cut into the Tower of London so he can steal the Crown Jewels. The villain leaves obvious clues (a distinctive button, a goose-feather) to distract Holmes (sending him— yes—on a Wild Goose Chase) so he can get on with his larger villainy undisturbed (an echo of the premise of the 1939 *Adventures of Sherlock Holmes*). Jerry, who wears a miniature Holmes outfit, catches on and thwarts the plot and Holmes makes some rapid deductions which bring him back to London to finish off the case. Tuffy (Kate Soucie), aka Nibbles, the baby mouse who is sometimes Jerry's nephew is oddly cast as a Barry Fitzgerald-type fighting Irish priest (Butch also gets an Irish accent) but is still a tiresome little ball of uselessness, while Droopy (Jeff Bergman) more aptly shows up as a plodding London bobby. Directed by Spike Brandt and Jeff Siergey.

✗

Kim Newman is a prolific, award-winning English writer and editor, who also acts, is a film critic, and a London broadcaster. Of his many novels and stories, one of the most famous is *Anno Dracula*.

MR. HOLMES

review by Lynne Stephens

The old poem erred; it will not always be 1895. In director Bill Condon's lyrical *Mr. Holmes* we meet our retired consulting detective caring for his bees in his seaside home in the austere but hopeful climate of 1947 post-war Britain. Watson's popular oeuvre of tidily-written "deerstalker, cape, and pipe" stories has cemented Holmes's reputation, but Watson was a massively unreliable narrator, rewriting cases's details and outcomes to suit the expectations of his avid readership. As Holmes rues, after the stories started to come out, "I had to play the part as Watson fashioned it!"

He's past all that now. Mrs. Hudson, John, and more recently Mycroft, have all passed on. Holmes lives simply, with his widowed housekeeper Mrs. Munro and her inquisitive pre-teen son Roger, who attaches himself to Holmes partly through fascination with Holmes's unique experiences, partly to bond with an adult male, and not least to assist him in building a life of intellectual stimulation rather than manual labor.

Holmes is failing, body and mind. Senility's tendrils strangle his short-term memory and erase entire sections of his past, leaving him in turns frustrated, frightened, and bewildered. But he's determined to succeed in one last challenging task: to recall the facts of his last professional case 30 years ago, an event so disastrous that afterwards Holmes abandoned his career and fled to East Sussex. "I chose exile for my punishment," he muses, "but what was it for?"

Based on Mitch Cullum's 2006 novel *A Slight Trick of the Mind* (some narrative events differ significantly between page and screen), *Mr. Holmes* artfully suggests that a life filled with gently crafted artifice may, ultimately, serve a kinder, longer-lasting purpose than the austere path of facts and logic. The "Sherlock Holmes" the public thinks it knows is actually a lifetime's accumulation of clichés and tropes from John's fictions, but would Holmes even be remembered had he not been packaged as an iconic, yet accessible, Victorian brand? In one scene, Holmes attends a "Sherlock Holmes" movie matinee and watches his on-screen alter ego (played in a tasty bit of "meta" casting by *Young Sherlock Holmes* star Nicholas Rowe) trounce eye-rolling vaudeville villains. The real-life Holmes disdainfully observes the melodrama, unrecognized and ignored by the movie-going audience.

Ian McKellen (*LOTR*, *Richard III*, Condon's *Gods and Monsters*) triumphs in the part of the aging Holmes, a lion in his winter. His is a highly physical performance built upon innumerable minute, meticulously rendered details, shifting from the shuffling, suffering 93-year-old to the feline confidence of the detective in his younger London prime. Milo Parker as young Roger winningly and soulfully holds his own in all his scenes opposite McKellen. Roger Allam (*The Queen*, radio's *Cabin Pressure*) and Phil Davis (BBC *Sherlock*) shine in cameo roles. Only Laura Linney's Mrs. Munro strikes a false note with a wandering accent and occasionally unreadable motivations.

The film's music, composed by Carter Burwell, creates a dreamy, melancholic mood completely in sync with the film's story and tone. English and elegiac in feel, *Mr. Holmes* graces us with a unique perspective on our beloved sleuth.

✗

Lynne Stephens' admiration for *Mr. Holmes's* Ian McKellen began in 1985, when she saw his now-legendary performance of *Coriolanus's* title role. Lynne works in marketing for cable television, and enjoys writing about travel and entertainment and everything British. She has been published in *The Washington Post*, *Starlog*, and *TheaterWeek*.

MATTERS MATHEMATICAL

by S. Brent Morris

I'm very well acquainted too with matters mathematical,
I understand equations, both the simple and quadratical,
About binomial theorem I'm teeming with a lot of news.
With many cheerful facts about the square of the hypotenuse.

Major General Stanley
Pirates of Penzance (1879)
W. S. Gilbert & A. Sullivan

Mathematics, to me, has always represented the pinnacle of the human mind, the achievements of pure, raw intellect. It is a form of expression that knows no bounds of time or culture. A mathematician today can communicate as well with a colleague on the other side of the world as with, if time travel were possible, a student from Aristotle's Lyceum. It is my opinion that God must be a mathematician. For if He said, *"Fiat Lux!"* on the first day, then surely He must have said *"Quod Erat Demonstrandum"* on the seventh. It is thus a source of professional embarrassment to me to see a mathematician leading the list of the foes of Sherlock Holmes.

Among the various nemeses faced by the great detective, only one has received from him the sobriquet of "the Napoleon of crime," and that was Professor James Moriarty. Holmes said further of him, "He is a genius, a philosopher, an abstract thinker. He has a brain of the first order." Little is known about Professor Moriarty, because "He [sat] motionless, like a spider in the center of its web." He did have a brother, Colonel Moriarty, curiously named James also.

And, to the point of this essay, he was a mathematical genius. We know that, "At the age of twenty-one he wrote a treatise upon the binomial theorem which had a European vogue. On the strength of it he won the mathematical chair at one of [the] smaller universities." This was not a major chair, like the Lucasian Chair of Mathematics at Cambridge, held by Isaac Newton nearly 400 years ago and by Stephen Hawking today, but it was recognition of significant achievement nonetheless. He was also "the celebrated author *of The Dynamics of an Asteroid*, a book which [ascended] to such rarefied heights of pure mathematics that it [was] said that there was no man in the scientific press capable of criticizing it."

A search of any standard history of mathematics does not yield the name James Moriarty, and *The Dynamics of an Asteroid* is conspicuous by its absence from the shelves of any libraries. It is indeed curious that a volume of this magnificent genius cannot be found. This absence of any record is perhaps testimony to Professor Moriarty's skill in staying behind the scenes. It could be, however, that his volume on *The Dynamics of an Asteroid* did not in fact ascend to rarefied heights of pure mathematics as Sherlock Holmes thought. If this is true, then we may have an explanation of why this exceptional mind abandoned the delights of mathematics.

Sir Isaac Newton solved what is known as the "Two Body Problem," that of calculating the orbit of one planet circling the sun. (In typical mathematician fashion, for his solution Newton assumed nothing else exists in the universe except these two bodies.) The "Three-Body Problem," that of two planets orbiting the sun, is now known to have no exact solution. That is, try as you might, be as complicated as you dare, you cannot express the answer with a single equation; any answer must involve numerical approximations—as accurate as you like, but approximations nonetheless.

Mathematicians today are well-versed in the existence of unsolvable problems, but not too long ago, it was thought that just a little more hard work would lead to success. The Greeks struggled with the problem of trisecting an angle with unmarked straightedge and compasses, but it was 2,000 years later that Erniste Galois showed that it simply cannot be done. Kurt Gödel rocked mathematics when he showed that every mathematical system complicated enough to be "interesting" must of necessity contain true theorems that cannot be proved within the system itself. But for mathematicians of the Victorian era, even for a genius like Isaac Newton from a far earlier period, the concept of an unsolvable problem didn't exist.

The dynamics of an asteroid of necessity involves the solution of the multi-body problem, more difficult even than the three-body problem. The location and velocity of the asteroid must be calculated with respect to the sun, planets, and other asteroids, and no closed form solution can exist.

Consider this scenario. Following on the success of his work on the binomial theorem, an overly confident Professor Moriarty publishes a treatise on this classic motion problem that falsely yielded a "closed form" or exact solution. Being a new professor at a small university, he would have raised funds for publication from friends and fellow faculty. And in the exuberance of youth he may have bragged more than a seasoned scientist would consider prudent. He may have had his eyes on a more prestigious chair, dare we even suggest the Lucasian Chair of Mathematics?

Moriarty's book would have been brilliantly written with but one small, fatal flaw that rendered the results useless. And we know now there must have been a flaw, because it is impossible to solve the three-body problem. This fatal flaw would have been overlooked by the initial reviewers, who lavished the book with praise. Moriarty's reputation from his paper on the binomial theorem could have blinded these first reviewers into thinking he had bested Isaac Newton. Then, after careful and tedious review by more senior mathematicians, the subtle flaw was found. An embarrassed Professor Moriarty would have had no choice but to purchase and burn all copies of the text (thus accounting for its absence from library shelves). He would have faced the considerable financial burden in repaying the publication advances of his friends. And if his *braggadocio* had gone too far for his Victorian academy, then he would have had no choice but to quietly resign his professorship and to retire to contemplate his vengeance on an unjust world. (Who among us hasn't felt the same rage after laboring all night over a math assignment, only then to discover the solution is wrong?) The shock and humiliation of publishing a wrong result, coupled with the financial burden of repaying advances, must have pushed poor James over the edge and led to his descent into a life of crime.

Sic transit gloria mathematica!

S. Brent Morris is managing editor of the *Scottish Rite Journal*, the largest-circulation Masonic magazine in the world. He has published widely on Freemasonry and in 2000 retired as a mathematician with the federal government. He has taught at Duke, Johns Hopkins, and George Washington Universities.

NOVEL VERSUS SCREENPLAY: HOW I LOVE THEE

by Lisa Cotoggio

When I think back, my love of writing began at the movies. As a child, I was drawn to the big screen, fixated, you might even say, but that was before I learned to read, of course.

Over the years it has become a tug of war—book/movie; movie/book. How can one decide? I couldn't, so I spend my days fluctuating back and forth, two screenplays to each novel, a progression that breaks up the monotony of the writing process.

A novel can be excruciating at times, the length, the time, the energy—sometimes it feels like the end will never come, but the screenplay's pace, intensity and shortness can help you stay focused and more quickly gain that sense of gratification we all desire.

Although there is nothing like that feeling of euphoria one gets when typing the words "The End" on the last page of your novel, the sense of accomplishment is just as great with that final "Fade Out."

Once again, it all comes down to choice. While I pen novels and screenplays, my approach to each is like night to day.

The screenplay is and always will be a visual piece, space is limited and you must choose your scenes carefully, but at the same time, character, action and story must take hold.

Screenwriting Tips:

- Read Syd Field, author of several screenwriting texts.

- Field suggests the use of index cards in three colors—thirty of each for beginning, middle, and end.

- In a screenplay, each part of the play (beginning, middle and end) must each, in turn, have a beginning, middle, and end.

- The plot point, or "twist," is where the writer pulls the beginning into the middle and your middle into the end, or climax.

I think if I had to choose, a novel, although longer, is much easier to write because length gives way to your imagination; it gives you flexibility to create and show more, to get inside the mind and thoughts of your characters, whereas a screenplay does not.

After my first novel, *A Spirit of Evil*, was published, I took on the task of writing the screenplay version of the story and I must admit it was one of the hardest things I've ever done. What to cut; what to keep—mind-boggling to say the least. Take three hundred pages and whack them down to one hundred and ten, give or take a few pages. You have to cut out all the narrative and internal dialogue so just the action remains. But you're not done—you then have to piece all the action back together because you only get to keep half of it. Which half, you ask? This is where the job really begins.

Craft, instinct and tools are important here. My tool of choice is *Movie Magic Screenwriter*. A pricey program, but well worth the investment. Unlike *Final Draft*, a program most screenwriters use, *Movie Magic* comes complete with a novel format and allows you to convert your manuscript into a screenplay. It saves time and cuts down on an already heavy workload.

Overall, I'd have to say the differences in writing a novel versus a screenplay creates a challenging experience for anyone willing to take on the job. I do it because it gives me an opportunity to cross genres; my novels are police procedurals, while my screenplays cross into action, drama and military/sci-fi. It's like having focus and freedom at the same time, and what writer wouldn't like that?

✗

A top ten finalist in the 2002 Nevada Film Office 15th Annual Screenwriting Award, Lisa Cotoggio has worked as a script doctor for Summer Moon Productions and with Classical Alliance as a TV series creator and writer.

A BRETON HOMECOMING (PART ONE)

by Peter James Quirk

1

On September 3, 1939, when Hitler's army marched into Poland, our peasant lives as we knew it ceased to exist. I remember sitting with the journalist Jean-Pierre Goldfeldt and his artist girlfriend Jacqueline listening to the radio when Great Britain and France declared war on Germany. We looked at each other with solemn faces and my friend and collaborator shook his head in disgust.

"That's the end of my book of your Breton legends, I guess, Padrig," he said. "I've got to get back to Paris."

He was gone by the end of the week. And the following week my fellow fisherman Young Yann joined a regiment that was forming at Vannes and after a short period of training he was sent to Verdun to guard the border. Like a good son, he wrote home every week and Old Yann showed me his letters while we were fishing.

Jean-Pierre also wrote to me several times. His editor sent him to Strasbourg to monitor the German frontier for any action that might unfold. But by the following spring, when Rommel's *Panzer* divisions began rolling into Luxembourg and Belgium, I lost track of him, although I assumed he was now moving with the army. Soon after that I ran into Jacqueline at the market and she told me he was back in Paris.

Over the next few weeks, my neighbor Alain and I listened in horror and disbelief to Jean-Pierre's radio as the whole Western Front collapsed and our once proud army scattered and fell back in disarray. The single bright spot that whole spring was the evacuation of the entire British Expeditionary Force, along with 80,000 French soldiers, by the British Navy.

They were snatched off the beaches at Dunkirk against terrible odds, while the *Luftwaffe* strafed them from the skies and the rear guard fought off the *Wehrmacht*. It had been, of course, a complete and utter defeat, but just the fact that so many men were saved—picked up and spirited across the Channel to England—was, to us, a miracle.

Meanwhile, the French Government fled from Paris to Tours and then to Bordeaux, then Daladier resigned and Pétain stepped in. He moved the Government to Vichy, sued for an Armistice with Germany and broke off relations with Great Britain. In retaliation, Britain recognized General De Gaulle as the head of the Free French and De Gaulle launched his famous radio appeal on June 18th—"France has lost a battle, not a war." Pétain condemned him to death immediately and signed an Armistice with Hitler.

Two weeks after the Germans arrived at the gates of Paris, they marched into Quimper, the nearest large town to my farmstead and the Breton people, angry and confused, braced themselves for Nazi occupation. As far as the official French government was concerned the war was over and during the next few weeks Breton soldiers, who marched off so proudly just six months before, began to straggle back to the region in twos and threes—filthy, hungry, and exhausted.

A frenzied banging from without brought me to my feet. A soaking rain had been falling for hours and I half-expected to find a patrol of bedraggled German soldiers on my doorstep seeking shelter. But when I pulled back the door, there was Old Yann, water streaming from tattered oilskins and the desperation of an anguished father etched on his weather-beaten face.

"What has happened to our boys?" he cried. "There has been no news. The airwaves are dead. What are we to think? What can we do?"

I quickly brought him in the house and helped pull off his oilskins. There was nothing to say or to ask, his face told me everything I needed to know and so I poured him a cognac and waited. He gulped twice at the fiery liquid, set down the glass and began to speak:

"I went down to Vannes yesterday to my son's regimental headquarters, but a German army unit has already taken over the building. Then, because most of his fellow soldiers come from that area, I walked around the town and harbor asking questions. But no one knows anything; none of the men are back yet. I don't know what to think."

"It's too early to worry," I said without conviction. "It's unlikely the entire regiment was captured. But, Yann, look at the bright side: perhaps he was rescued at Dunkirk and now he's sitting in some English public house drinking warm beer. How could he get word to you from there?"

The possibility of young Yann being in England brightened his mood considerably and I promised to monitor the Free French radio broadcasts for him. But when he returned later, it was he who brought news: "Some men from his regiment are back," he said excitedly. "One of them brought a message to me. My son is alive!"

"Thank you, Mother of God!" I said as I crossed my heart in supplication. "Where is he? Is he a prisoner?"

"No, but he was wounded; he took a bullet in the leg. His friends carried him as far as Nantes, and now he's hiding at a doctor's house getting treatment. I have the address. We just have to go and find him and bring him home."

"And just how do you propose we do that? We can't just go and fetch him on the train; he's a wounded soldier. The Germans would simply pick him up and send him off to prison camp and we'd probably be put up against the nearest wall and shot."

"No, Padrig. Not the train—the boat. We'll go get him with the boat. They can't stop us fishing. We'll sail down the coast and if we see a German patrol boat, we'll just throw our nets in the water."

"You think we can just sail down to Nantes in an eighteen-foot sailing dinghy in the middle of a war!" I said, shaking my head. "Have you thought it through?"

Yann nodded his head vigorously. "Sure," he said. "It'll be easy. Those *Boches* aren't so smart. They lost the last war, didn't they?"

I was silent for a few minutes while I thought it over. He hadn't even asked if I was willing to go with him. He just assumed that as a member of his crew and an old friend, I would do whatever he wanted—sail into hell, if need be. But I guess he was right. I had known him since the First War and I'd watched Young Yann grow up, fished alongside him since he was seven-years-old. If Yann needed me to help save his son—how could I refuse? It was just a matter of how and when.

"It's going to take at least five days to get to Nantes and back," I mused, almost to myself. "That means I have to ask Alain to feed my livestock." I looked at Yann: "Are they issuing fishing permits yet? We're going to need some form of identification. There'll be patrol boats everywhere."

"Come down to the harbor as soon as you can," he replied. "I'll take care of the permits. Oh, and when you talk to Alain, don't tell him any more than you have to. He can't tell the Nazis what he doesn't know."

I looked up sharply. "Don't you trust him?"

"We don't know who to trust yet," he replied. "The war has only just arrived here. Nobody has had time to choose sides. Just don't tell him anything he doesn't need to know."

When Yann left, I walked with him as far as my neighbor's farm. But when I stopped beside the gate and turned toward him, he grasped my wrists, his face choked with emotion:

"Listen, Padrig. I... I... this means a lot... he's my only son.... Mother of God, you know what I'm trying to say." Then, his arms dropped to his sides, his face softened and his eyes teared up for a second before he was able to control his emotions. He then nodded his head and turned back down the road.

When the door to Alain's house opened, an eight-year-old girl stood before me, a solemn expression on her face and a finger held up to her lips:

Shhh," she whispered. "Poppa and Momma are listening to the Free French broadcast from England. We have to be quiet."

I smiled grimly. Alain and his wife Jeanne-Marie had seven children and I could only imagine what dire threats it took to keep them all quiet for fifteen minutes. I walked in and was waved to a seat.

"De Gaulle's calling for massive resistance against the invader," said Jeanne-Marie. "Whatever we can do—anything from civil disobedience to armed insurrection. But it's hopeless. What does he expect? What would happen to the children if we were shot or sent to prison?"

I realized then that Yann was right. Everyone's priorities were different and until they committed to the cause you couldn't say a word and especially not in front of children. I stood up and motioned to her husband.

"Alain," I said. "I've got to find something in Jean-Pierre's cottage. Can you open the door for me?"

"It's open," he said. "His girlfriend is staying there."

That's better yet, I thought, as I walked across the yard.

When I knocked on the cottage door, Jacqueline was also listening to the Free French broadcast, but her mood was markedly different to that of her neighbors. When she saw me, she leapt out of her chair and ran to my arms:

"Oh, Padrig," she cried. "Our France, our beautiful homeland: there are no words to describe my feelings. The sight of these strangers—these Nazi soldiers—marching around on the sacred soil of our ancestors makes my skin crawl. For my family back east it makes two times in the last twenty-five years. But what can we do? The pigs are everywhere!"

I held her closely as I tried to console her. "I know, Jacqueline, I know," I said, softly. "But we have to be patient. We can't be hasty and do something stupid that gets us shot in the first week of the occupation. We have to sit back and size up the situation. And when we know who our allies are, then maybe we can do something."

I pulled away from her gently and she stood there, her body heaving with silent sobs.

"Listen carefully, Jacqueline," I said as she wiped her eyes. "There is something you can do. I have to go away for a few days. Can you feed my livestock?"

She studied my face carefully. "May I ask where you're going?" she said slowly. I shook my head and a tiny smile touched her lips. "I thought not. Yes—count me in, my friend—my comrade."

Then her features hardened again as another thought crossed her mind. "Have you heard from Jean-Pierre?"

The question took me by surprise. "Not since the invasion. Is he still in Paris?"

"I don't know; I haven't heard from him, either, and I'm getting worried. I hear they've been rounding up Jews and deporting them to labor camps in Germany."

"Jean-Pierre is well aware of that," I replied. "He's not just going to walk up to them and surrender. If he has no other option, he'll make his way back to Brittany. Trust me, Jacqueline. Here he can melt into the landscape as our first Jewish Breton peasant, and if he learns to speak Breton, he can pretend he doesn't speak French and he can hide out indefinitely working the land or fishing with Yann."

The next morning while riding down to the harbor, I was dragged from my bicycle and searched by an enemy patrol just outside Kérity. On that cloudless summer day, I received an abrupt demonstration of the weight and the consequences of Nazi occupation. We Breton peasants were still struggling against the abuses of the landowners and their minions 150 years after the revolution, and my body convulsed in silent rage as I watched any gains we might have made goose-step away in gray uniforms.

I met Yann on the wharf and he brought me up to date: "A company of *Boches* marched into town yesterday. They bivouacked in the schoolhouse and took over the village hall."

"Is it complete chaos?"

"No. I stopped by there this morning; it's really not that bad. Luckily for us they kept the village secretary and she told me they would be issuing fishing permits tomorrow. We have to get one for the boat and one for each crew member. But there's a catch. Each man has to go down to the hall and get his own."

"Can't she give us an extra pass for Young Yann?"

"She said that each pass has to be stamped individually by the officer in charge. There's no way around it."

I cursed them roundly and spat on the ground. However, those very acts of frustration gave me the seeds of an idea and I told Yann I would work on a solution that evening and meet him outside the hall in the morning. Then I rode back to my farmstead and spent the remainder of the day showing Jacqueline around the property. But in the evening over dinner, I explained our new situation and the dilemma we faced. She was receptive, even enthusiastic to my rough-hewn plan and offered some suggestions. But the next day outside Kérity Village Hall she was not so sure:

"How do I look?" she asked for the tenth time. She was wearing Jean-Pierre's wool sweater and oilskins, an old pair of clogs and her long flowing hair was crammed up into my navy-blue fishing cap.

"Perfect," I said, reassuringly. "It's as though we just pulled in the nets. But remember, when we get inside, stand behind Yann and pretend you don't speak French. I'll do all the talking."

"Let's go over this one more time," she said. "You want me to walk in there, pretend I'm Yann's son and pick up his fishing pass. Don't you think the secretary, what's her name again? Anna?

Don't you think that Anna doesn't know who he is? Won't she realize we're trying to fool her?"

"You don't have to worry about Anna," I replied. "She knows Yann's away in the army. But she can't ask the Nazis for three passes if there are only two men standing by her desk."

"And I just stand there looking dumb?"

"No, not dumb—inconspicuous. You're just a fisherman who suddenly needs a pass so he can continue to make his living. Believe me, Jacqueline, we'll be in and out of there in no time—the quicker the better."

Jacqueline was silent for a moment as she quelled her demons, then she smiled and nodded: "Okay, Padrig, my raconteur, my wonderful storyteller," she said as she grasped my arm. "Let's get it done before these damn clogs cripple me permanently."

2

"**D**o you think they're going to search our boats?"

"Did you remember to bring your ID?"

We were, perhaps, twenty strong, fishermen all, sitting in the harbor cafe waiting for the morning tide to turn. Yann sat across the table from me, tight-lipped, jaw set, hunched over his coffee. One could only speculate what was on his mind as we prepared to sail into the unknown. I, on the other hand, tried not to think about it and I contemplated the room, listening to fragments of conversation.

Just two months earlier, men such as these would have been animated, good-natured, as they discussed the weather, the price of fish, their families. But now, they were confused, angry, resentful—the Nazi jackboot was suddenly a cruel reality in their daily lives.

ACHTUNG! screamed a notice on the cafe door—a warning to a vanquished people that for every German soldier found assassinated, ten civilians would be selected, taken to the nearest wall and shot.

But out in the harbor, Yann's boat, the *Kenavo*, was ready, straining against her moorings, impatient to be underway—to take a stand—to show these strutting peacocks that if taking our land had been easy, holding onto it was going to be a long bumpy ride.

Yann glanced at the wall clock. The morning tide had begun to ebb and soon dozens of boats would be pulling out of the harbor and heading for their secret fishing grounds. We wanted to be part of that exodus.

"Okay," he said, finally. "It's time." He nodded toward the other men as they gathered their equipment and marched toward the door.

Once outside the cafe, I heaved my duffel onto my shoulder and crossed the road to the jetty where the crowd stalled at the top of stone steps. Barring the way was a German sergeant armed to the teeth and bolstered by a squad of infantrymen standing off to his left.

"You must show me your identity cards," he barked in halting French, in response to any and all questions posed.

I eased toward the front of the crowd to watch the drama unfold. The sergeant's expression was tense—anxious—and so were those of his men. The fishermen, however, were beginning to enjoy his inability to speak Breton and were making no attempt to respond in French. They didn't seem to realize the gravity of the situation—that they could be shot in an instant. Even Yann had a smirk on his lips.

I dug an elbow into his ribs. "Yann," I warned. "He's losing his patience. If we aren't careful, someone's going to get hurt."

Yann quickly came to his senses. "You're right," he said. "Those *Boches* look ready to start shooting. You'd better see what you can do."

I nodded, took a deep breath and stepped out of the crowd. *"Guten Morgen, mein Herr,"* I said, using my entire German vocabulary to draw his attention. To my surprise, his demeanor relaxed immediately, which, in turn, reassured his men. Behind me I could hear Yann calming the fishermen and I was reminded of the awesome powers of reason and diplomacy. I held out my arms in a vague gesture of appeasement and continued: "No, Sergeant, I don't speak German, but, unlike my compatriots, I do speak passable French. Would you like me to act as an interpreter?"

He was as relieved as I was to break the tension and it wasn't long before everyone received the Third Reich's authorization to pursue the only livelihood they had ever known. Mine was the last ID to be returned and with his task complete, the German sergeant came over to thank me for my assistance. There was an uncomfortable pause, after which he held out his hand.

What was I to do now? Ignore the outstretched hand and risk being shot? Or did I shake it and face the wrath of my friends, my countrymen?

Once again, diplomacy saved the day: "Listen, Sergeant," I said, quietly. "I was glad to help you back there. I don't want to see people getting shot for little or no reason. But for all that, we are still on opposing sides and I hope you will forgive me if I don't shake your hand. I'm still going to be living here long after you've gone home."

"I quite understand," he replied. "I'm not a regular soldier, either. I, too, would prefer to be back with my wife, my family and my friends. Good luck with your fishing." With that, the offending hand became a wave and the sergeant turned back to his men.

Once we cleared the harbor entrance, we raised the sail and made for the open sea. "Take her out a ways," called Yann after he had scanned the horizon, "then steer a course for the Iles de Glénan. We need to stay away from the mainland as much as possible."

"If we island-hop all the way down the coast we should stay out of trouble," I agreed.

Yann nodded grimly. "The *Boches* have only just got here. They couldn't possibly have had time to establish control of every community. The smaller islands probably aren't even occupied yet. There must be fifty of them in the Gulf of Morbihan alone." His eyes swept the skyline one more time. "At least the weather's good. If it stays like this, we can keep going all night."

That seemed a tad optimistic. "I don't know about that," I countered. "The *Boches* are not stupid. If they see a boat they don't recognize sailing down the coast in the middle of the night, they would probably blow it out of the water just for target practice—especially when we get near the big naval bases like Lorient or St. Nazaire."

Yann's face tightened a little; he didn't like unsolicited advice. But he relented a little and shared his thoughts: "I know we can't do much about St. Nazaire," he replied. "It's on the mouth of the river.

But we can stay away from Lorient. We'll head for Groix. I want to sail into one of the tiny fishing harbors there and look around. You never know, we may learn something we can use later."

The island of Groix, which was located just west of the entrance to Lorient harbor, was well visible from the mainland. But it was far enough away, we hoped, that we wouldn't excite any patrol boats. That was the theory. But as we sailed farther down the coast it became apparent that the venerable old seaport, laid out by Colbert in the Seventeenth Century, figured quite prominently in German naval strategy. There was much activity, both in and out of the estuary.

We were still some three leagues away from Groix when we had our first shipboard encounter with the enemy. A gunboat came roaring out of Lorient and bore down on us at high speed. At first we feared she was going to plow right into us, but at the last moment she veered to starboard and cut her engines.

She circled around us several times as she slowed down, while her grinning captain and crew inspected us for weapons. And when the gunboat finally pulled in beside us, the captain leaned over from the bridge, lifted a megaphone to his lips and called out in Teutonic-accented French:

"Ahoy there, *Kenavo*. Where are you from and what is your business?"

Yann, who was livid from the near collision, shrugged his shoulders and pointed to the fishing nets: "Drop dead, you useless pile of dogshit," he called back in Breton. We both smiled and waved.

Plainly puzzled, the captain frowned and pointed to our name. "What does *Kenavo* mean?"

"Goodbye, "I replied. "We're fishermen out of Kérity, just west of here."

"Do you know you need a permit to be out here?"

I nodded and patted my breast pocket. Apparently this and the fact that we were clearly non-threatening, seemed to satisfy him. He nodded back, lowered his megaphone and barked an order in German. The gunboat pulled away and headed back to Lorient.

I turned to my companion. "That was pretty stupid. If he understood what you said, we'd both be dead by now."

"There aren't many Frenchmen who speak Breton. Where the hell would they find a *Boche*?"

"Listen, I'm here because I want to help you bring your boy home. I don't want to die because you can't hide your feelings or hold your tongue. There are lots of things we can do to get rid of these pigs, but shouting insults at them in Breton is just useless bravado."

Yann's response was a loud snort and a look of complete scorn; then he busied himself raising the sail again. I grasped the tiller and turned the boat back into the wind and once more we set out toward Groix. We knew on the leeward side of the island there were several tiny fishing harbors we could enter. In one of those, we hoped, we could get something to eat and drink and maybe rest up for the night without causing too much commotion.

Toward the end of the second day, the *Kenavo* entered the Loire River estuary and sailed past the provisional German fortifications at St. Nazaire without arousing any overt curiosity. We continued upstream toward Nantes through river traffic, which, surprisingly, was quite heavy, despite the recent incursion and I suggested to my captain that we should perhaps take advantage of our engine.

By way of response, Yann, who had been sitting in the bow studying the buoys and landmarks and comparing them to his dog-eared river chart, got to his feet and began lowering the sheet. He came aft to help me to lift our outboard over the stern and clamp it down. Then he stowed the canvas while I primed the pump and began coaxing the motor to life. After a few wheezes and sputters we were under way again and it was not long before the spires, towers, and jetties of Nantes came into focus off the starboard bow.

"Shall we pull in, make fast to a pier and just ask for directions?" asked Yann as he studied the shoreline. "I'm not familiar with Nantes."

"We don't have much choice," I replied, with a shrug. "But let's continue upstream and make note of likely moorings. And when we come about, we can tie up at the most promising one."

About an hour later I cut the motor and we drifted in beside a run-down jetty. And after securing our lines to metal bollards, we climbed back on board to eat the last of our provisions.

"Do you know where we are exactly?" asked Yann, as he reached for the cider jug.

I shook my head. "I've only been here once or twice. Shall we make a foray into town?"

"I don't think we should leave the boat unguarded," he replied. "You don't need me with you."

While that was certainly true, there wasn't much an unarmed Breton fisherman who spoke neither French nor German could do to protect the boat, either. But I wasn't about to remind him of that; so I kept my thoughts to myself and prepared to disembark.

At that moment, the roar of an engine brought us to our feet. And as our eyes scoured the waterfront, a motorcycle and sidecar turned onto the dock from between two abandoned warehouses. It roared up to the jetty and the soldier astride the machine, a splendidly-attired cavalryman replete with helmet, jodhpurs, and black-leather gaiters, dismounted and unclipped a sub-machine gun from beneath the handlebars. He held it loosely but kept it aimed in our general direction as the man in the sidecar, a ranking officer, stepped out and pulled himself erect beside him.

"Don't do or say anything stupid," I warned my volatile companion. "Our story is plausible. I just need to stay alive long enough to tell it."

At that moment, the officer, a major, called out in fluent French: "Step down from the boat and put your hands on your heads. Then walk toward us slowly."

As we climbed down to the dock and my back was turned to the Nazis, I whispered nervously to my companion: "Be really careful, Yann. The officer speaks very good French."

"Where are you from and what is your business?" demanded the major as approached.

To be continued . . .

✗

Peter James Quirk is an author, freelance writer and outdoorsman who spends his winters skiing and snowboarding and his summers hiking, biking and playing tennis. His novel *Trail of Vengeance* has a strong ski theme; indeed, the villain of the story is a disgraced ski instructor. Many of his stories, however, cover World War II and its aftermath. It is a fascinating if tragic period to explore, and the villains and heroes are so easy to find.

THE ADVENTURE OF THE COPPER BREECHLOADS

by Zakariah Johnson

PREFACE

History records that on 5 May, 1887, the famous American sharpshooter, Annie Oakley, then touring London with William "Buffalo Bill" Cody's Wild West, created a minor diplomatic stir. When presented to the Prince and Princess of Wales following a command performance for the royal family, Miss Oakley reached out and shook Princess Alexandra's hand before shaking Prince Edward's. The royal couple laughed off the American's faux pas, and the tittering in the press about American social graces (or lack thereof) soon abated. However, Miss Oakley's choice of hands was quite deliberate, and had nothing whatsoever to do with etiquette; a fact about which the press remained, happily, ignorant.

It was half-past ten in the morning on the first Monday in May; the dawn clatter of hansoms and mongers had faded from the street outside the window and had not yet been replaced by the noon rush. I had been called on an early round that morning and, having returned, was drawing as much pleasure as possible out of a tepid cup of coffee while my friend Sherlock Holmes sat before me at the table, using a mirror to examine marks on his neck with a pair of precision calipers.

"Is it still troubling you, Holmes?" I asked. "Would you like another salve?" It had scarcely been a week since Holmes had narrowly avoided death by strangulation at the hands of J. P. and Alec Cunningham, a villainous father-son pair whom Holmes had exposed in the murder of their servant, events I related in *The Adventure of the Reigate Squire*.

"It's these bruises, do you see, Watson?" Holmes replied, craning his neck toward me. His vocal cords had been temporarily damaged by the strong hands of the younger Cunningham and he spoke with a severe rasp, rather like an extreme Flemish accent. "What does medical science have to offer on an unusual ratio of digits with the coincidence of mental abnormalities?"

"Digits? I take it you mean fingers?"

"Quite so," he said, continuing with his measuring, touching his hand gingerly to his throat, which was clearly still sensitive.

"Nothing definitive on the subject," I admitted. "Certain abnormalities of the hand sometimes appear in conjunction with other infirmities, sometimes alone. Heredity plays a strong role, of course. What prompts your interest?"

"These hand prints so generously left on my neck by Alec Cunningham indicate his index fingers are longer than his ring fingers. I had noticed something singular about his hands when we first made his acquaintance, but of course my mind was on other things when I had the opportunity for closer study. The bruises may not be true to the hands that made them, but it would be interesting to confirm it. It would be interesting as well to see if the same pattern appears in his equally criminal father. Perhaps I can arrange to measure their hands after they are hanged for William Kirwan's murder."

"You suspect a link between their physical aberrations and their criminal mindset?"

"It is a leap to theorize from a sample size of one; or even two, should the elder Cunningham prove to carry the trait as well; but there are other indications—Paganini, for instance."

"Now really, Holmes, your Paganini was more a prodigy and a virtuoso than the opposite. Surely you would not cite his famous abilities as evidence for your theory on the hands of murderers?"

"Perhaps, but consider, Watson; Paganini's life was overburdened with evidence of impulsiveness strikingly similar to the weaknesses of criminality—his gambling and scandals of the heart. It was not just for his unearthly skill on the violin that he became known as the 'witch's child.' However, I can support no theories with him, because I have no information about the ratio of his digits to each other, only that they were universally noted as prodigiously long, a trait I can but hope is not indicative of any substantial mental failings." With this he set down his calipers and with a smile held the backs of his own long-fingered hands up for my inspection.

Before I could reply, further reveries on data sets and the physical manifestations of mental aberration were interrupted by our landlady, who brought in with her a diminutive woman I took at first to be an adolescent dressed in the most remarkable outfit. The stranger stood barely five feet tall, and was slight but firm in her build, certainly not frail despite my initial perception of girlhood. Her wide-brimmed hat was flat at the crown, more suited for a teamster than a Victorian lady. Her white dress was modest in all regards, with a collar rising to her chin and long sleeves covered at the ends by leather gloves. Her dress was much shorter than the style common in those days—before these so-called "flappers" we see now—reaching just below the knee, and ending in tassels that encircled the hem all the way around. She carried a matching white umbrella in her left hand. Despite her short height, she wore flat, simple but sturdy shoes that added nothing to her stature but that let her walk forward with a quicker gait than one is accustomed to with women who wear their normal footwear. Her face was round, which was emphasized by the way she wore her long brown hair pulled straight back. She didn't speak as Mrs Hudson introduced her as "Mrs Butler" and then retired, but from the first she seemed nearly bursting with energy, as if she might bound across the room and shake my lapels at any moment.

Holmes rose, a sudden twinkle in his eye. He wrapped a silk scarf around his neck to cover the bruises and extended a hand to the young woman as Mrs Hudson closed the door on her way out.

"Sherlock Holmes, at your service... Mrs Butler, was it?"

"Mrs Frank Butler," she replied as she took his hand in a firm grip. "But most people call me Missie." Her accent marked her as American, something her dress should have told me. But not a New Yorker or southerner, something altogether different. On closer examination I saw she wore little make-up and the lines in the corners of her eyes showed she was older than I had first thought, indicating as well an outdoor life to go along with her esoteric attire.

"Mrs Butler," Holmes replied, rasping slightly. "This is my associate, Dr Watson. Please forgive my voice; I've had some unexpected injuries lately."

"Are they ever expected?" she asked.

"Quite right," Holmes assented, indicating she should take the couch before her, he and I each taking our chairs opposite. "Now, what can I do for you, Mrs Butler? Or should I say, Miss Oakley?"

"Annie Oakley?" I exclaimed. "The markswoman with Bill Cody's *Wild West*?"

"Of course, Watson; though that is a stage name. Can you fail to recognize the face and, excuse me, Miss, the clothes that currently festoon every spare inch of wall or fence throughout the whole city of London?" As ever, Holmes's powers of observation were correct, though, in my defense, those ubiquitous poster advertisements he spoke of did nothing to convey the vitality and sheer force of personality that was her defining characteristic. "I believe the show opens to the general public on the ninth, correct, Mrs Butler?"

"Yes, May 9," she said. "But that's not what I'm here about."

"Of course not," said Holmes, leaning back in his chair and bringing the tips of his fingers together on his chin. "Why don't you tell me about your little problem then?"

She looked at him for a few moments as if she were about to say something unpleasant, then changed her demeanour and began her tale. "It's not *my* problem, Mr Holmes. It's not even an American problem. It's a British problem, a very British problem if ever there was one. I've been in London a little over a month as we prepare to open the exhibition. Other than practicing, I don't have a lot of duties to perform, so I've taken to giving lessons to ladies at one of your gun clubs here in London."

"Lessons in what? Not shooting surely?" Holmes interjected.

"And why not? It's perfectly proper. Every woman should know how to defend herself, no matter her station. And any lady who doesn't enjoy a day in the field with her dog and her husband shooting birds and taking in the air doesn't know what she's missing. Besides," she added, almost under her breath, "some women would do better to find ways to keep an eye on their... dogs."

"Pardon my interruption. Please continue," Holmes said.

"Well," she went on, "I've been giving lessons, mostly to your gentried types. Yesterday there was this... Harry... in our group. A nice kid. Good shot, too. After we'd taken some quail, the two of us had tea and I could see Harry was distressed about something.

Eventually… he opened up and told me a terrible story about… his mother losing her wedding ring. Apparently Harry's father is, well, there's no easy way to say this," she blushed profusely, "Harry's father is a bit free with the ladies for a married gentleman. Far too free, if you ask me. Harry's mother has heard stories but this time things seemed to have gotten out of hand and she went to her husband's—'friend'—and confronted her. They had some strong words and this lady, Harry's mother, took off her wedding ring and threw it at the other before rushing out in tears. A few days later she contacted the other woman to get the ring back and was told its return would cost her a small fortune, more than the ring was worth. Also that if she didn't pay up the ring would be released to the right vultures to create a scandal."

"Her husband's 'friend,' is she willing to risk exposing herself in this manner?"

"That's what Harry was on about. It isn't in the lady's character to do so. Exposure would ruin her as surely as anyone in this affair. Harry suspects she's had her arm twisted to get her to go along with the game."

"The passages of the lower and even middle classes, no matter how salacious, are rarely tracked by our esteemed press. What is the woman's name?"

"I can't mention Harry's mother's name, I made a promise about that, but I can tell you the other woman's name." Miss Oakley fairly spit the name of a woman of renown who moved in the highest circles at the time.

"But surely you can't mean—" I began.

"Not a word, Watson," Holmes broke in. "Mrs Butler… Miss Oakley—what shall we call you?"

"Missie works."

"Missie," Holmes said with difficulty, "Miss Oakley, has this 'Harry' asked you to work as agent in this regard to affect the return of the wedding ring?"

"Yes."

"Then allow Watson and me to work as yours. I can see what you are unable to tell me, what we must leave unspoken. You can trust that we will not fail you, and we may require your help."

"Count on me, Mr Holmes. I respect a man willing to stand up to the wolves that prey on the lambs of this world. I've found there are far too many of them."

"Too many wolves or too many lambs?" Holmes asked.

"Exactly," she said.

Miss Oakley left soon thereafter, leaving Holmes in an agitation such as I had rarely seen him.

"Holmes," I said. "You surprise me. Sordid as this episode proves to be, I hardly believed you would ever deign to apply your talents to such purely domestic trifles."

"Domestic, Watson? No, I only wish it were so. Indeed, there will be *international* repercussions if we cannot set things right and soon. Miss Oakley is said to be a woman of many talents, but prevarication is, perhaps to her credit, not among them. Her story about 'Harry' was transparently false, but not so false that I couldn't see at once to whom she was referring."

"You know Harry's identity?"

"Both Harry and the mother, as I'm sure you will discern in your own time if you merely apply yourself. It's a bad business, Watson. I only hope we can do something in time."

✗ ✗ ✗ ✗

I had already spent most of April out of town, and as I had to occasionally pay my creditors, I was gone from Baker Street on medical rounds until late in the afternoon. I returned to find Holmes gone but Miss Oakley in attendance, at work hemming the shirt cuff of the most extraordinary gentleman I had yet laid eyes on. He had thick, curly hair reaching past his shoulders, a pointed beard and a wide, flowing moustache to be envied by the Merovingian kings of old. He was my height, a bit shorter than Holmes, but solidly built. His thick riding boots reached above his knees and he wore a blood red shirt embroidered with flowers a less masculine male might have hesitated to wear. His neck was wrapped in the famous silk scarf of the American plains and the broad hat on his head was wide enough to double as an umbrella.

"I'd say you could only be William Cody," I exclaimed, stepping forward to shake his hand. "Dr Watson, at your service!"

"A pleasure, Doc!" he said firmly seizing my hand; his voice was rough after the character of American plainsmen. "We were told you would return soon." His grin froze on his face for a second or two as I wondered what to say next, then I saw mischief creep into those grey eyes I knew all-too-well.

"Holmes!" I said and the three of us fell into laughter.

"Thank you for that," Holmes said at last.

"But that accent, it's perfect!"

"The sole benefit of my recent injury, I assure you. If I can fool even you for a few seconds, I'm confident no one else will be the wiser. As you can see, it's fortunate Mr Cody is known to wear a scarf, so I can hide the marks on my neck without attracting attention to it. Thank you for the alterations, Miss Oakley."

"Not at all," she said, putting her supplies into a handbag. "I'd say even Bill's friends might be fooled, at least from a distance."

"Then that's all I can hope for when I visit our blackmailer this evening. Fortunately, I had no trouble making an appointment, since she clearly expected some third party to be contacting her."

"But why make such a ruse, Holmes?" I asked. "Surely you don't have to worry about your own exposure since the object of the meeting is to haggle over payment?"

"If I thought for a moment the lady in question had thought up this plan on her own, I would not hesitate to agree with you, Watson. For her to act so recklessly suggests there is another party controlling our negotiations, and for that reason I prefer to retain anonymity in the matter."

"The bird that doesn't flush is never fired on," said Miss Oakley.

"Precisely," said Holmes.

✗　✗　✗　✗

Holmes returned quite late in the evening, breezing in with his great coat covering up the outlandish costume he had borrowed from the unknowing Buffalo Bill. It was long after Miss Oakley had returned to the great tent city near Earls Court, where the *Wild West* had encamped in order to have their animals near their performance arena. She had said she would be engaged with another private shooting party in the morning, followed by her daily target practice with her husband, but would return to Baker Street the following afternoon to learn Holmes's discoveries.

Holmes threw himself down before the same vanity mirror and began to apply solvent on a cotton swab to remove the false moustache and beard.

"It is worse than I feared, Watson," he said. "The lady has indeed become a pawn in a larger game, one intended to embarrass people who ought not be put up for public humiliation."

"What price did she name for the ring?"

"Price? What price, indeed? I doubt she knows its true price, in blood or treasure. When I first arrived in the guise of Cody acting as Harry's agent it seemed natural to her that no Englishman had been sent to negotiate. What does that tell you, Watson? She attempted to hide the truth, but soon enough broke down and told me everything. Once she had possession of the ring, she set off at once to find a certain agent here in town—a rascal named Hugo Oberstein—who had been blackmailing her with worse exposures than she risks now. I tell you, this current masquerade of mine is nothing compared to those performed around us daily!"

"So she stands to gain nothing from this business?"

"Nothing beyond the return of some lurid tintypes she should never have posed for," he said, throwing down his beard in disgust. "But the agent, yes, he knows full well the value of what he has. I have managed to keep our names and Miss Oakley's—Mrs Butler's—dark, but that may not be possible forever. Our soiled dove will deliver a message to Oberstein tonight, naming Cody as the negotiator he has to deal with. The reply will be delivered to Mrs Butler's Red Indian friend as arranged. Since his English is limited and he is a presumed illiterate, our agent should feel secure in sending his reply to 'Cody' through this gentleman, though naturally the real Cody will never see it."

"Do you foresee any danger to Buffalo Bill in this?"

"I doubt it. He is constantly surrounded—supervising the exhibition by day and feted by night. Our advantage is that his meetings with the 'gentried types,' as she put it, are not public events. This keeps him out of the way. If it is eventually discovered there was an imposter, all the better for Cody's safety that he knows nothing about it."

"How do you propose to get the money from Harry for negotiations?"

"I do not propose to get any money at all! We may despise the common swindler, Watson, but reserve your worst judgments for the agent who would send men to their graves in the thousands by shifting the balance of power in the world for the sake of a few hundred thousand pounds—pounds that I will not place into his hand."

"Surely the situation isn't as bad as all that?" I said.

Holmes said nothing, but by way of answer set two heavy tumblers on the table and filled them with more whiskey than was our usual measure.

⚹　⚹　⚹　⚹

The following evening was unseasonably warm as I returned to Baker Street following dinner alone at my club. Holmes and Miss Oakley were at work on the already too-cluttered floor fitting a two-foot-long map-carrying tube over the end of a small-bore rifle.

"Ah, Watson, you're just in time," said Holmes, standing and helping Miss Oakley to her feet. "How's the weight?"

She held the rifle out from her. I saw it was designed so she could hold the butt firmly against her shoulder and sight down the barrel without bending her neck at all. However, the added length of the map tube made it difficult for her to hold.

"I can still see my target," she said, as she took mock aim at various treasures around the room, "but there's no way I can shoot like you want me to with the extra weight on the end."

"As long as you can see, the bipod on the hansom will take care of the weight."

"Holmes, what is all this?" I asked. "Are you expecting to extend the range of this rifle with a longer barrel?"

"Not at all. Miss Oakley's skills will extend the range as far as is needed. This crude addition is to keep her role in this evening's adventure quiet. Now, if you'll grab that putty from the table, we can fasten it properly."

I grabbed the putty and brought it to them. Holmes took a finger full and began applying it around the base of the tube to hold it fast. "If you were to hold the rifle, Watson, you'd notice the device is heavier than it looks. The tube is filled with wire mesh surrounded by cotton rags I've treated with chemicals to prevent their ignition from the hot gases expelled when the rifle fires. Those same rags will absorb the sound. You've loaded the bullets as I asked?"

"Right here." She reached into the pocket of her knee-skirt and pulled out six short, bright copper bullets, each no bigger around than a pencil. "In our performances I'm used to shooting light loads for the protection of the crowd, but I don't know if your tube will mess up the trajectory."

"Then let's find out."

Holmes walked to the window and pulled it open. "Stand near the rear wall and load the rifle, please." Holmes walked over in front of Miss Oakley where she stood against the rear wall. She released the lever and the barrel bent downward in the manner of a shotgun, forming an inverted V with the stock. She pushed one of the tiny cartridges into the breech and snapped it closed. Holmes stooped down in front of her and reached behind him to rest the map tube on his left shoulder.

"Now... do you see the spot of red paint on the brick just to the right of the window across the street?" Holmes asked.

"Yes."

"Shoot it."

"Bend down a little more." Holmes did as she asked. Moments later there was a click as the hammer hit the shell and a light pop of the primer but I heard nothing else.

"It appears we have a misfire," I said.

"The paint says otherwise," said Holmes.

I rushed to the window and looked across the street. "But the spot is still there, Holmes."

"Use the spyglass."

Doing as he said, I took up the spyglass set on the lintel and looked again. In the dead middle of the red dot was a smaller circle of white and gray where the bullet had struck.

"Unbelievable," I said, turning to face them. Miss Oakley broke open the gun to reload. "I barely heard a sound!"

"Let's hope that Oberstein is similarly impressed," said Holmes. "Hurry then, we've got little time."

✗   ✗   ✗   ✗

Darkness found me hiding behind a curtain in the dining room of a large home east of Earls Court. The house had been closed up when the owners left the previous autumn for business abroad that Holmes did not describe. My hand stayed put on the butt of the service revolver in my coat pocket, but Holmes sat placidly at the long table in the middle of the room lit only by a five-candled candelabra he had insisted on bringing, since the gas in the house was inoperable. The windows on opposite ends of the long table were both opened, as if to let in a cross-breeze for the unseasonable heat.

The candles had burned down about halfway when I heard the noise of the front door opening and several pairs of heavy footsteps thumped with assurance through the hall. The door to the dining room was open, and without delay three men walked into the room, two of them quite large. The third man was of a more average size and came last into the room, his attendants standing to each side of him.

"Mr Cody, I presume?" said the third man, walking toward the table with his hand extended.

"Sit down, sir," said Holmes in an accent so replete with the sound of prairie winds that the candles before him might have been a campfire surrounded by teepees. "I have no time for pleasantries or any desire to engage in them. We are here about business. Let's get on with it."

"As you like," said Oberstein, taking the chair opposite Holmes, a slight lisp heightening his viper-like demeanour. His men stood to either side of him, surveying the room. "You have full authority to act in this matter?"

"It's as I stated to you. You will get your rewards once I have the ring. Show me."

"Surely you can't expect me to—"

"Damn it, man, show me the ring or this meeting is over."

"Very well. I trust there will be no trickery, since your client has more to lose than I do by police involvement." He reached into his pocket and produced a small box. Holding it in both hands, he held it close to his chest as he opened it. "As an American, you may not understand what it would mean were this to appear on the continent, Mr Cody. But I assure you, the lady you work for does. Did you bring the money? I don't see it."

Holmes laid his hands in front of him on the table and then raised his index fingers. At that instant the candle nearest to him suddenly went out as a sound like a tiny bee passed through the room. Oberstein appeared not to understand what had happened.

"I'm sorry you don't see clearly, Mr Oberstein," said Holmes. "Perhaps it's on account of the dark?" His raised his middle fingers. At that instant the second-nearest candle went out. Oberstein's men began looking around.

"What is this, Mr Cody? Surely you don't want the police involved? We three did not come alone. I could leave this instant if I chose."

"Could you?" said Holmes, putting the tips of his outstretched fingers together. The middle candle went out immediately as a *whizz* passed between the men. "If you think you could walk out of here, I invite you to try."

Holmes crossed the fingers of his hands together and the fourth candle went out an instant later. Oberstein stared at him across the table, his mouth gaping.

"Perhaps you would like your men to wait outside while we finish negotiating?"

Oberstein twitched his head to the side and his two men walked backwards out of the room.

"Close the door!" he snapped. It shut quietly. Holmes then reached out and took the last candle from the candelabra and relit the other four with it before returning it to its base.

Holmes spoke softly, his rasping voice raised barely above a whisper. "Now." I pulled the gaudy kerchief over my face and pulled my hat down low as I stepped out from behind the curtain, revolver in hand. "I'm glad you're intelligent enough to realize your position, Mr Oberstein. The umbrella stand in the hall contains enough money for you to pay your men and save face, but nothing else for your efforts." Holmes held out his hand. "The ring."

Oberstein stood up and flexed his hands at his sides. "I will ruin Mrs — for this!" he hissed, naming the woman who had first taken the ring.

"That's not my concern. The ring!" Holmes held out his hand, his eyes boring into Oberstein as I walked up behind our prey with my pistol at his back. With a snort, Oberstein reached into his coat, pulled out the ring and slammed it on the table. Holmes snatched it up and was on his feet at once. "I suggest you stay put for five minutes, Oberstein. If you attempt to leave this room before that, you'll be still forever." With that we both dashed to the far window and went out feet first, silently lowering ourselves to the ground.

"Quickly!" Holmes said as we dashed around the corner of the house. A shadow stepped forward from behind a tree and Holmes lashed out at once with his riding crop, knocking the gun from the man's hand. A second later, I dropped him with a blow to the head with my revolver and we soon made it to the tall yew hedge at the back of the property.

Breaking through the hedge, we saw Miss Oakley standing on top of the hansom, wrapped from head to toe in tight black clothes that hid her almost entirely. Her rifle was positioned over a bipod affixed to the rear, which had given her the support she needed to shoot out the candles.

"Come on!" she said. "They're coming!" Holmes was quickly at the reins, Miss Oakley sitting between us. He snapped the reins and the horse shot forward.

Miss Oakley handed me her rifle. "Rip that thing off! I can't shoot it without support!" I struggled to twist the map tube and break the putty holding it in place while hanging on in the narrow seat at the same time. We heard the shouts of men coming from around the hedge as we pulled out of the gravel side lane and into the main road.

A pistol shot rang out and a bullet passed over our heads.

"So much for stealth," said Holmes in his normal voice. "Watson, can you dissuade our pursuers?" Now a full volley of shots rang out behind us and I turned to see an open carriage with four men in it pulled by a full team quickly closing the distance between us.

"Grab my feet!" yelled Miss Oakley. Without waiting, she turned and crawled onto the roof of the carriage. The hansom was jostling on the uneven road as Holmes hurried our horse. I turned and threw my weight onto her legs to keep her from falling off, only hoping I could manage to stay on as well. Lying prone, she aimed the small rifle and fired. It made barely more noise than it had with Holmes's contraption over the end, but I glanced up in time to see a hat fly off the head of one of the men in the pursuing carriage. She quickly reloaded and fired again, to the same effect. With the third shot, the hat came off of the man driving the team— who apparently put together the correlation between his de-hatting and the popping of the little breech-loader—and the team slowed, though not to a complete halt.

"The camp is just ahead," said Holmes, as Miss Oakley and I regained out seats. He reached into his pocket and pulled out the ring. "I trust you can determine the best manner of returning this?" he said as he passed it to her.

"I'll figure something out," she said.

"Good," said Holmes. He glanced over his shoulder. "I see our pursuers are still with us, if from a distance. If you were going to leave unnoticed, the grove ahead would be your best bet." He put the reins into his left hand and held out his right. "Until next time, Missie."

"Until next time, Mr Holmes." She shook his hand and then nodded to me. "Dr Watson." I leaned back and she brought her left arm and leg over me as she spun from the center of the seat to the outer edge, then spun again and wheeled off the speeding hansom into the brush and into the trees without stopping. At Holmes's insistence, I resisted the urge to turn and check on her safety, but when I did turn I noticed the carriage following us, now far behind, had passed the spot she had disembarked without slowing.

"Time, I think, Watson, for us to end this chase." There was more traffic on the road now as we headed toward central London and after several high-speed turns that nearly pitched me out of the seat, we ourselves vanished into the crowded heart of the city, a hansom in a sea of hansoms, until we were able to return the vehicle to its owner, far from Earls Court.

✗ ✗ ✗ ✗

Obtuse though Holmes finds me at times, that Thursday I didn't require his guidance to ascertain from the evening newspapers that Annie had returned the wedding ring to its rightful owner, Princess Alexandra, wife of Prince Edward, who became Edward VII, our late sovereign, by passing it to her when she shook her gloved hand following the command performance of Cody's *Wild West*. "Harry" was of course a family nickname for the headstrong Princess

Maud, now queen of Norway, who had taken up the challenge of regaining the ring after her mother had confided in her of her father's infidelities. It might seem strange or imprudent to share such details of marriage with one's child, but with whom else should the great lady have shared the heartbreak that so frequently attended her? Still, though I cannot condone his actions toward his wife, I prefer to look after the beam in my own eye rather than condemn our late king, whose famed liberality and greatness of spirit led him to treat rich and poor, black and white as one and the same in the bosom of his humanity; a liberality that unfortunately extended as well to the married and the unmarried, his own status as the former notwithstanding. I dare say even Holmes would agree that history provides ample data to support my thesis that such pain as Alexandra endured has often correlated with marriages made for alliances between states rather than for love.

Despite the nearly four decades that have passed since that May in 1887 and the subsequent deaths of most of the principals, I remained honour-bound for Holmes's release before telling of the incident. The recent passing of Annie Oakley, followed quickly by the death of her beloved husband, reminded me of these singular events and led me to telegram Holmes of my desire to at long last tell the tale. He answered succinctly with the message, "It can't hurt now," which is his usual response to such queries these days. Though such reticence on his part could as likely indicate he is ardently pursuing other matters as it could indicate a depressive torpor, I shall resolve to visit my friend in person once the current rains again lift their curtain from London and the chill from this old soldier's bones.

✗

Zakariah Johnson is a writer and book editor living in coastal New Hampshire, and a member of the Portsmouth Writers Salon. His crime and mystery fiction has appeared in *Danse Macabre*, *Shotgun Honey*, and *Yellow Mama*; with other stories pending. Zakariah zealously reads and re-reads both the original Holmes canon and any pastiches he can latch his mitts on, sharing both around the dinner table with his growing brood.

PAROLE VIOLATOR

by Laird Long

Don Bradford checked his watch—12:35. Ervin Rudd still hadn't appeared at the dented red metal door of the Boulevard Hotel.

"Wake up, sleeping beauty," Bradford muttered to himself, sitting in his car by the curb.

A bum stumbling by on the sidewalk glanced at him. It was a hot day, and Bradford had all the windows open. He stared back at the bum, and the guy shuffled on down the cracked sidewalk with a broken-tooth grin and a wave of his dirty hand. Just as Rudd pushed through the door of the hotel across the street and walked out onto the sun-blasted sidewalk.

Bradford didn't have to look at the picture cut out of the newspaper he'd been given. He easily recognized Rudd's long, lean, wolf's face, the shaggy black hair and slouched shoulders. The man's height and weight matched up with the rest of his physical description, as well. Completing the positive ID was the paleness of Rudd's face—not a hint of tan despite the summer sunshine. A jailbird, fresh out of the pen.

Rudd squinted and put a bony hand up to his bony brow. He glanced briefly at Bradford's car, but it didn't mean anything to the ex-con. He'd served half of a ten-year sentence for killing a man, was out on statuary parole. His obligation to society was now merely to report in with his parole agent on a regular basis, and appear to stay clean.

Rudd scrubbed a finger under his nose and hunched his shoulders, then loped on down the sidewalk. Bradford keyed his car to life and rolled after the man.

There were all kinds of amusements for a guy just out of the joint, on Front Street. Bars, massage parlours, boozcans, crack houses, shooting galleries, pool halls, gambling dens, prostitutes on patrol almost every hour of the day and night. Rudd obviously had a thirst on from too many years swilling cell-made shine, because he cut across Broad Street and shoved through the door of the Occidental Beverage Room on the corner.

Bradford cruised on down Front, found a parking spot and pulled in. He turned off the car's engine, then checked the gun tucked away in his jacket pocket. He got out of the car and crossed Front, pushed into the bar.

It was cool and beery inside. Bradford let his eyes adjust to the gloom, walking slowly into the big room. There were dark, round tables and red, padded chairs laid out on the floor, a stripper stage thrusting out into the middle from the far wall. There were only ten or so men scattered around the room, nursing beers and watching the Asian exotic dancer grind out her moves up on the stage. Rudd was sitting at a table by himself alongside the platform, a pitcher of beer and a glass in front of him.

"Wanna try the buffet?"

Bradford turned his head and glanced at the fat man in the food-stained white shirt standing behind a buffet set-up against the near wall. Piles of chicken wings and a couple of logs of meatloaf shone greasily under the heat lamps.

Bradford shook his head, said, "Gimme a beer." Then he sat down at a table far from the stage.

He sipped his watery beer and watched his quarry, looking for an opening. But there were just too few witnesses, the place too dark, for Bradford to make his move. So, he waited patiently. Until, just after one-thirty, Rudd finally unfolded his lanky form and got to his feet, stretched like a contented animal.

Bradford hadn't moved from his seat the entire time. Now, he jumped up just as Rudd arose, was out the door of the bar before Rudd had even turned to look in his direction. Bradford jogged across Front Street back to his car, the bright sun blinding and dizzying him, for a moment.

Rudd slipped out of the bar and proceeded on down the sidewalk, heading north. He covered two blocks, then stopped at the Aragon Pool Hall between Smith and Rutland on Front. He looked around, nervous like all newly sprung cons, then jerked the battered aluminium door of the joint open and slipped inside.

Bradford stopped at a red light, then pulled into a parking spot just beyond the intersection. The day had gotten even hotter, and he was sweating under his jacket. But his hard face was impassive, his strong jaw set, his blue eyes cold. He'd been on many such shadow and surveillance missions when he'd been a cop, and he knew that if he just played it cool, he'd come upon the perfect opportunity to nail Ervin Rudd. It was just a matter of patience, steely nerves, and grim determination—then swift and violent action when the opening presented itself.

Bradford exited his vehicle and crossed Front Street, pulled open the aluminium door and entered the Aragon Pool Hall.

Rudd was bent over a green felt-covered table at the back of the smoky-smelling room, shooting a stick at a white ball, lit up by the bank of lights hanging over the pool table. He was playing against another man, a short, round guy with a shiny moonface.

The man was jabbering away, as Rudd slammed a red ball into a corner pocket.

There were two pairs of men at two of the other tables, a threesome at another. There were ten pool tables in all, a few scattered card tables and chairs in front of the snack bar next to the door. The men playing snooker and billiards were heavy-set and bearded, dressed in dusty blue jeans and black leather vests. Biker types.

Bradford didn't like this set-up, either, as he surveyed it. It was the kind of place where all sorts of things happened that went unreported, were covered up; and these were the types of men who kept their mouths shut, especially around cops.

"Want a table?"

Bradford glanced at the dark-skinned dwarf perched up on the stool behind the snack counter. "No, thanks. Just sight-seeing." He turned and left the building, crossed the street back to his car and settled in for another wait.

Rudd re-emerged just after four. He stood on the sidewalk and straightened out a crumpled ball of bills, then glanced sharply around and shoved the money into his jeans. He was on the move again, loping down Front Street still headed north.

Bradford pulled out of his parking spot and slowly followed, like a shark cruising a swimmer. He shifted over into the boulevard lane. The sun beat down on the car. It was an oven inside. But Bradford was undeterred, a man on a mission.

Rudd turned left onto Graham Avenue, just before Front plunged into an underpass and popped up again into a low income residential district on the other side. Bradford sat out the light in the left-hand turn lane, watching Rudd snake through a group of exiting customers and into the Shanghai Express restaurant.

Bradford turned onto Graham. He had to drive two blocks down the street before he could find a spot to park. City Hall was close by, and things got busy this time of the day. He jumped out of his car and jogged back up Graham, pulled open the two sets of glass doors and went into the restaurant, anxious not to lose Rudd now that he'd put in all this hot trail time.

He needn't have worried. And this time, the set-up was perfect.

A grim smile creased Bradford's pressed lips. He wiped sweat off his broad forehead with a swipe of his big hand.

"Just one, sir?"

"Just one," Bradford replied to the gaunt Chinese guy manning the service lectern. "I'll find a table myself."

The restaurant was half-full, some sort of office function taking place in the middle of the long room, a series of tables pushed together sideways. There were pairs and groups of other patrons, mostly seniors and civil servants off early. The dinner buffet opened at four.

Bradford adjusted his jacket, checked the gun in his pocket. These were good, clean, honest citizens who would make credible witnesses and wouldn't hesitate to call the police, pitch in themselves in an emergency. And the room was well-lit. Rudd was sitting at a two-chair table against the far wall, a pair of plates loaded with Chinese food in front of him. He was wolfing the food down.

Bradford weaved his way through the cheaply-decorated room, past tables of happily chattering customers. Until he came to the table next to Rudd's against the wall. He yanked out a chair, slamming the back of it into the back of Rudd's chair.

The man jumped, choked on an eggroll. He twisted his head around and glared up at Bradford. "Hey, what the fuck!?" he angrily spluttered batter and bean sprouts.

Bradford grinned, humped his chair back a bit. Then he took a step even closer to Rudd and looked over the man's bony shoulder. His heavy, booted right foot landed on Rudd's light canvas sneaker.

"That looks pretty good," Bradford said, leaning over Rudd and looking down at the man's plates of food, pressing his foot hard into Rudd's foot, putting almost all of his weight into it.

Rudd's wolf face burned red, his knuckles flaring white gripping his knife and fork. "What the fuck you doin'!?" he rasped in a strangled voice, his eyes popping and a purple vein leaping to beating life on his bony forehead.

"I just said that looks pretty good," Bradford repeated, grinding his boot into Rudd's sneaker, piling on the pressure.

He knew Rudd had a hair-trigger temper. That's why he'd killed Mike Tomko, when the little man hadn't handed over his wallet quick enough for Rudd's liking. It was those so-called 'anger management issues,' and the fact that Rudd had pistol-whipped Tomko with his .38 instead of shooting the man, that had allowed Rudd to plea-bargain a second-degree murder rap down to manslaughter; get away with only a ten-year sentence reduced down to half under statutory release provisions.

"Get your fuckin' foot off!" he snarled at Bradford, trying in vain to pull his injured foot away from Bradford's crushing boot.

The hair-trigger temper hadn't gone anywhere, despite the 're-habilitation' programs.

Bradford slowly lifted his foot up, still grinning. Rudd jerked his leg away, his right hand rising with the knife. No one else in the restaurant had noticed the incident, Bradford's bulky body screening the scene.

"Just saying," Bradford said pleasantly to Rudd. Then he turned his back on the man and walked over to the line at the buffet, picked a plate up off the stack.

He glanced briefly back at Rudd. The man was watching him, his eyes narrowed and his face frozen in hate. The table was set, Bradford figured. All he needed to do now was serve up the main course. Cold revenge.

He walked back to his table, balancing a food-laden plate in one hand and a hot cup of tea in the other. Rudd's wolf's eyes watched him every step of the way, the man twisted around in his chair. When Bradford was within three paces, his foot accidentally-on-purpose caught on the carpet. He tripped, stumbled forward, his cup and plate thrusting precariously up into the air.

Rudd's eyes went wide and his mouth dropped open. He threw up his arms, protecting himself from what looked like certain catastrophe, as Bradford lunged at him unbalanced.

But the big man easily jumped to a stop, steadied himself, two feet away from where Rudd sat startled and staring. Bradford smoothly brought his cup and plate back down to chest level. Then, looking Rudd square in the eye, he leaned over and spat into Rudd's half-eaten plate of food.

Rudd gaped, stunned. Bradford grinned.

The ex-con exploded, pushed past the point of control for a man of limited self-control. He leapt up from his chair with a roar and slammed his fists into Bradford's broad chest.

"Hey, what are you doing!?" Bradford innocently yelled out, tossing the cup and plate back over his head and staggering backwards with more than a hint of theatrics. Crockery shattered in a violent blast of noise, and food and drink splattered everywhere. A family of three at a nearby table took the brunt of the sharding china and drenching liquid and eats while Bradford's big body banged into another table where a couple of women had been pleasantly dining, sending the table rocking and clattering, setting the women to screaming.

Rudd charged at Bradford. Bradford set his feet and grabbed onto Rudd's shoulders, as Rudd pounded away at his chest and stomach. Shrieks and shouts filled the electrified air, as the men grappled, one obviously beating at the other, all eyes focused on the pair.

Bradford wrestled Rudd back closer to the wall, using his superior strength and training. Rudd pummelled Bradford's ribs, his mouth and nose foaming.

When they were back alongside Rudd's table again, Bradford pulled his right hand off Rudd's left shoulder and shot a short, vicious jab into Rudd's stomach. The man blew food and saliva, jerking over. Bradford quickly slammed his fist up into Rudd's jaw, knocking the man back against the table, dazed. It all happened so fast.

"Call the police! He's got a gun!" Bradford yelled over his shoulder at the crowd, sitting Rudd down in his chair. He covertly dove his hand into his jacket pocket and came out with the cold .38, dumped it into Rudd's lap.

Then he jumped back, pulling the semi-conscious man forward so that the gun clattered onto the floor, as Rudd's body sprawled out like he had slipped. The gun was the same make and model that Rudd had used in the pistol-whipping murder of Mike Tomko.

In the ensuing pandemonium, heroic citizens sprang forward and kicked the gun away from Rudd, jumped on top of the stunned man and pinned him to the floor *en masse*. As others frantically punched 911 on their cellphones, Bradford quietly slipped away from the yelling and gesticulating crowd and right out of the restaurant.

Back in his car parked on Graham Avenue, Bradford used his own cellphone. "It's been all arranged, Mrs. Tomko," he said, hearing the sirens already wailing down Front Street. "He'll be arrested for causing a disturbance, busted for possessing a stolen weapon; his parole violated and the scumbag sent back to prison to serve out his full term."

"Thank God!" Mrs. Tomko exhaled. "Thank *you*!"

Bradford heard her swallow, hard. "It just wasn't fair… that he killed my husband and got away with such a light sentence. That he got out early on parole. I—I had to—"

"I know, Mrs. Tomko. Don't worry, it's done." Bradford paused, letting the woman catch her breath. "You can mail the remaining $2,500 to the post office box number I gave you."

"Yes, yes, of course! I… it just wasn't—"

"I agree, Mrs. Tomko," Bradford cut her off, watching the flashing blue and red lights in his rearview mirror, as police cars skidded up to the curb and the crowd in front of the Shanghai Express. "Sometimes justice has to be… forced."

He tossed the cellphone onto the seat and keyed his car to life and pulled away, a grim smile on his hard face.

✗

Long pounds out fiction in all genres. Big guy, sense of humour. Writing credits include: *Blue Murder Magazine, Hardboiled, Thriller UK, Shred of Evidence, Bullet, Albedo One, Baen's Universe, Woman's World, The Weekly News, that's life!, Sherlock Holmes Mystery Magazine, The Forensic Examiner*, and stories in the anthologies *Amazing Heroes, The Mammoth Book of New Comic Fantasy, The Mammoth Book of Jacobean Whodunits*, and *The Mammoth Book of Perfect Crimes and Impossible Mysteries*.

THE DISCOVERY

by Meg Opperman

"Since I know that you will be pleased at the great success with which the Lord has crowned my voyage, I write to inform you how in thirty-three days I crossed from the Canary Islands to the Indies. ...I found very many islands with large populations and took possession of them all... this I did by proclamation and unfurled the royal standard. No opposition was offered."

—Christopher Columbus
(Letters to Various People, First Voyage)

The day Professor Robert Carson lectured in my *psicologia* class, I almost missed it. I was recovering from a migraine, and my body ached like I was coming down with a flu. But I was a good girl. The first *muchacha* in my family to go to the university. *Universidad Central de Venezuela*. Lots of expectations and hopes riding on me.

He was fit, tall, American. The face of an *ángel*. A Fulbright scholar, I learned later. Such passion. Such knowledge. All of us—young, yearning—under his spell.

After class that day, my friend, Marianela—bold to a fault—went to ask the handsome *gringo* a question, and I trailed behind, too shy to ask one myself. Too young to even know that I should question.

The American scholar answered my friend absently, a gentle smile on his open face. He turned to me.

"You have beautiful eyes," he said. "I see the fire of Venezuela in them."

I blushed. Surprised. Pleased.

✗   ✗   ✗   ✗

"In order to win their friendship, since I knew they were a people to be converted and won to our holy

> *faith by love and friendship rather than by force, I gave some of them red caps and glass beads which they hung around their necks, also many other trifles. These things pleased them greatly and they became marvelously friendly...."*
>
> —Christopher Columbus,
> (Log Book, First Voyage)

Robert and I married that next October, my classes forgotten.

"Such a special day," he said when we set the date.

I laughed. "Of course, *mi amor*. A wedding day is always special."

He seemed to consider this wisdom. "Perhaps. Did you know it's also a holiday in the U.S.?"

"Really?" I said, eager to hear more about America. "Which one?"

"Columbus Day," he said, surprising me by pulling a lovely gold necklace from his pocket. He draped it around my neck. "A perfect fit."

Then he swung me around, and, breathless, I forgot the questions I wanted to ask.

✗ ✗ ✗ ✗

> *"The sea is very smooth, thanks to God, and the breeze very agreeable."*
>
> —Christopher Columbus
> (Log Book, First Voyage)

At the wedding, my family so proud. My father, he cried. My mother, she fussed. My grandmother, she prayed. My dress pressed and my veil straightened. Suitcases packed. Ready for America.

"Are you sure, Celeste? Really sure?" Marianela asked a week before my wedding.

"*Sí*, of course." How arrogant! How jealous! She wanted my happiness. The life I'd live with Robert in Washington, D.C. In America. To hurt her, I said, "Everything's *perfecto*. Just perfect."

✗ ✗ ✗ ✗

"May it please Our Lord to forgive the persons who have libeled and do libel this noble enterprise and who oppose and have opposed its progress without considering what honour and glory it brings to your royal estate throughout the world."

—Christopher Columbus
(Letters, Third Voyage)

America is cold. Cold weather. Cold people. Nothing like the warmth of Venezuela. No one comes to visit. No one on the street stops to ask how I am or even makes eye contact. It's like I don't exist in Robert's world. Like the awful cold is shrinking me and soon I'll fade away. Robert says to give it time; two years isn't enough. He tells me to be patient. To learn more about his culture before I can expect to have friends.

But what of our neighbors? Not one has come to our lonesome house in Woodley Park with its cavernous rooms and stone staircases. Our spacious foyer gone to waste. No welcome party. Invites for coffee. Oh, how I miss my native coffee beans! (Robert says Venezuelan coffee is too expensive and without taste, that I must learn to drink that acidic Columbian mud that he favors.)

The houses here are so close, I can open our windows and almost touch my neighbors's homes. Yet there is so much distance, it's as though Robert and I live in the most remote of places. All of us living in our beautiful shells, decaying inside.

Shivering, I clutch my coat tightly and hurry to catch my bus. Class tonight. History.

✗   ✗   ✗   ✗

"Most of the day was calm, but there was some wind later."

—Christopher Columbus
(Digest of Columbus's Log Book, First Voyage)

Gracias *Diosito*! I've made a new friend. Paulina is Ecuadorian and also misses her homeland. She lives with her daughter and cleans houses during the day. She works for the Bauers two houses down. I don't know them, but I see Mr. and Mrs. Bauer leaving in the morning, both in suits and driving expensive cars. I've said hello a few times, but they always pretend they don't hear me. And maybe they don't. Some days I don't know if I can hear myself.

Paulina reminds me of my mother. Round, but dignified. We talk of our families and make jokes that Americans wouldn't understand. I invite her to my place for coffee, but she won't come.

"Ah no, *Señora* Celeste. I clean peoples's homes, but I don't live there." She smiles when she says this, maybe thinking to soften the blow.

It stings.

✗ ✗ ✗ ✗

> *"They should be good servants and very intelligent, for I have observed that they soon repeat anything that is said to them, and I believe that they would easily be made Christians, for they appeared to me to have no religion."*
> —Christopher Columbus
> (Digest of Columbus's Log Book, First Voyage)

I don't like history. No, not so much. The past is the past. Salvation lies in our present and future, my grandmother always said. I think of her more and more these days. Her wise words and tender guidance. Learning the Rosary when I was a girl, my grandmother's calloused hands caressing the beads with the gentlest of intentions, explaining the importance of prayer. I suppose that is a history of sorts, isn't it? The passing down from one hand to the next, generations of ritual and behavior. I hadn't considered that before.

The History of the Americas 1400-1800 was not my choice. Robert felt I needed to learn more about his people's great accomplishments. And some were great. *Sí*. But the books tell many lies, too. These thoughts I didn't share with Robert. He wouldn't approve. Would again call me ignorant and laugh in his genial way to take the bite from his words.

I'd wanted to go to American University, Robert's university, but he says I'm not ready. My English not good enough. My brain, too untutored. An embarrassment to him still. So I attend

Montgomery College. One class. Grateful to be out of that solitary house two days a week.

During the last session, I met two classmates. Perhaps in time, they will be friends. A girl, my age, with a Mendoza surname who doesn't speak a word of Spanish, and a boy named Jamal who says he can't afford a university.

I get up the courage to ask them, "Would you like to go for coffee after class?"

✗   ✗   ✗   ✗

> *"I gave many gifts to the Quibian, as the chief of the country is called, but I knew that friendly relations would not continue for long, since they were very uncivilized and our men preemptory and I had taken possession of land in his territory."*
>
> —Christopher Columbus
> (Letter to the Spanish Sovereigns, Fourth Voyage)

We sit at some coffee chain, learning about each other. No Venezuelan beans, but Jamal recommends a Kenyan blend that's pleasing.

It feels good to talk about Caracas. About my family, my brothers, my little sister. Both my new friends are so eager to learn about my homeland. And for once, I ask lots of questions. Why doesn't Anne—with a surname of Mendoza—speak Spanish? Where had Jamal grown up? What was Southeast D.C. like?

After a time, my phone rings.

"Where are you?" Robert says, breathless.

"I'm having coffee with friends I met in class."

"I've been so worried. Come home." His voice pleading, but something steely underneath.

"Of course, *mi amor*. I'll come now."

✗   ✗   ✗   ✗

> *"I had his canoe hauled aboard also and all that he carried kept safe. I ordered that he should be given bread and honey and something to drink. I shall carry him to Fernandina and restore all his possessions to him so that he may give a good account of*

us. Then when, God willing, your Highnesses send
others here, we shall be favourably received and
the natives may give us of all they possess."
—Christopher Columbus
(Digest of Columbus's Log Book, First Voyage)

The next night, my movements are slow and pained. I don the long-sleeved, black dress Robert bought me last Christmas. I prefer something shorter in the sleeve and hem, but Robert says American women wear tasteless fashions and I mustn't fall under their influence.

A dinner in Georgetown with some of his colleagues. Boring old men and dried-up women who talk of nothing but the mind.

But always I go.

I wrap my neck in a colorful scarf my grandmother sent from home—I mean, from Caracas—America is my home now, Robert says. The fabric beautifully woven with colors that remind me of our outdoor markets. Vibrant and free. My grandmother has chosen well. The scarf conceals the worst of the bruises.

Reaching into a hand-carved box, I sort through the gold jewelry and select Robert's latest apology. I fasten the thin bracelet around my wrist.

This time, he also adds five kilos of Meridas—Venezuela's finest coffee. So I wouldn't need to go anywhere—like a coffee shop—to experience the smells and tastes of Caracas. It's to be enjoyed at home.

⚹　⚹　⚹　⚹

"Although the villages are very close together,
each has a different language and consequently the
people of one do not understand those of another,
any more than we understand the Arabs."
—Christopher Columbus
(Letter to the Spanish Sovereigns)

This morning, Paulina sits on the Bauers's steps, having a quick smoke. If she won't come to my kitchen, I will bring my coffee to her.

Marching over, I hand Paulina a steaming cup of Meridas. I've added cream and sugar to make it extra sweet.

Paulina looks at me like I'm crazy, but takes a sip. And I feel gratitude toward this woman who speaks to me, always says hello.

"Your bracelet is lovely," she says. "So delicate."

"From my husband," I say.

She nods, but her eyes wander to my neck. I adjust my turtleneck self-consciously.

✗　✗　✗　✗

> *"The Indians reported that many other ships had arrived at Paria and in the Carib islands and afterwards came the news of six other caravels brought by a brother of the chief magistrate, but these reports were malicious."*
>
> —Christopher Columbus
> (Letter to the Governess of Don Juan, Third Voyage)

I do not enjoy class this week. My stomach aches, and I feel the beginning of a migraine. Anne and Jamal ask me to go for coffee again, but I tell them I can't.

After class I hurry to catch my bus. It's delayed, and when I walk through the door, Robert calls to me from upstairs. His voice echoes in the foyer.

Slowly, I climb the slick stone steps, grasping the bannister for support. For a moment, I consider throwing myself over its rail, feeling the air give way as I plummet toward the cold tile floor.

Reaching the top, I creep down the hallway, see the bedroom door standing ajar. I don't enter, my feet frozen in place.

From behind me, Robert says, "You're late."

I turn. He's not smiling now.

✗　✗　✗　✗

> *"This was the native village of the man I had found on the previous day with his canoe in mid-channel. He had given such a good account of us that canoes swarmed round the ship all that night. They brought us water and something of all they had. I ordered presents to be given to all of them, that is*

*to say, strings of ten or a dozen small glass beads
and some brass clappers of a kind that are worth a
maravedi each in Castile…"*

—Christopher Columbus
(Digest of Columbus's Log Book, First Voyage)

A few days later, I see Paulina sitting on the Bauers's porch, enjoying her cigarette. I pour two cups of Meridas, add the cream and sugar.

"Here, Paulina," I say. "Enjoy."

She sets her cup down, seems to look hard at my face.

Did I not wear enough make up? I sip my coffee, pretending I don't notice.

"New earrings," she says. "Your husband again?"

I blush, touch the elegant gold bands. "He loves me very much."

Paulina begins to say something, but reaches for her cup instead. She takes a sip, then says, "Even hot coffee cools over time."

But she's wrong. It scalds.

✗ ✗ ✗ ✗

*"One, Adrian, led another uprising at this time but
the Lord did not allow him to effect his evil purpose. I had made up my mind not to harm a hair
on anyone's head, but unhappily on account of his
ingratitude I could not spare him as I intended."*

—Christopher Columbus
(Letter to the Governess of Don Juan, Third Voyage)

Robert comes home from work early tonight. He's smiling and gives me a hug. Holds me close.

"Ah, Celeste. You're so beautiful." He strokes one of my earrings, then trails his finger across my chin.

I smile back, basking in his approval. Just like our early days.

Then he stiffens.

I look where his gaze has settled. Two empty coffee cups in the sink.

"Who was here, Celeste?"

"No one, *mi amor*. I took coffee to the Bauers's cleaning lady. She is from Ecuador—"

He puts a finger to my lips, steps back. Going to the sink, he picks up the cups and hurls them both against the wall.

⚡ ⚡ ⚡ ⚡

"They have no religion and I think that they would be very quickly Christianized, for they have a very ready understanding."
—Christopher Columbus
(Digest of Columbus's Log Book, First Voyage)

I miss a week of classes. Study at home. I speak to no one but Robert. One evening, our phone rings, echoing throughout the cavernous rooms.

So desperate to hear someone else's voice—even a wrong number—I pick up the receiver. "Hello," I say. "The Carsons's residence. May I help you?"

Jamal's voice says, "Celeste? You okay? Anne and I were worried when you didn't show up this week."

"Yes, I'm fine. I just had a flu."

"Anne and I are meeting Monday at the same coffee shop, so we can study for the midterm. You wanna come?"

"That's Columbus Day," I say, at a loss.

"Uh, yeah. I guess. We're meeting at noon, but will probably stay and have dinner in the area. You in?"

"I can't, Jamal. Columbus Day is sort of my wedding anniversary." I laugh nervously. "I mean, we married two years ago on Columbus Day, so it's still a special day for us."

Jamal sounds disappointed. He hangs up. I grip the phone to my ear, wishing I could say so much more. That's when I hear the click as someone else hangs up the phone, too.

⚡ ⚡ ⚡ ⚡

"I was in the Plains and the adelantado was where this man Adrian had raised a revolt, but things were now settled, and the country rich and at peace."
—Christopher Columbus
(Letter to the Governess of Don Juan, Third Voyage)

I see Paulina entering the Bauers's home, no time for a cigarette today. I stand on my porch, jacket wrapped tightly to keep out the cold. I wait, a cup of coffee cooling in my hand. Today, I am going to confide in her. I will tell her about Robert-who-gives-me-gold-but-does-not-love-me. I will tell her all of it.

When she exits the Bauers's, I call to her.

She does not look in my direction. Keeps walking. Her face a series of angry lines.

I run to catch up. "Paulina, wait. I hoped we could talk."

She turns to me, but her face does not change. "Your *gringo* almost had me fired, *Señora* Celeste. He says I am spending my time with you instead of cleaning."

I don't know what to say.

She walks away, with only a single glance over her shoulder.

Is that pity in her eyes? I don't feel the cold any more. Only the heat of my anger.

✗   ✗   ✗   ✗

> *"Eyes never saw the sea so rough, so ugly or so seething with foam. The wind did not allow us to go ahead or give us a chance of running, nor did it allow us to shelter under any headland. There I was held in those seas turned to blood, boiling like a cauldron on a mighty fire."*
> —Christopher Columbus
> (Letters to the Sovereigns of Spain, Fourth Voyage)

Columbus Day. I've called Jamal back. Told him I'll be coming to the coffee shop after all.

As I get ready to go, Robert walks into our bedroom. He's come home from work early again.

"Celeste." He crooks his finger at me, knowing I'll come. His smile gentle. "I've a gift for you."

I approach him, wary.

From his pocket he pulls a gold necklace, thick and clunky. Not like the other pieces he's bought. He places it around my neck and it pinches a little.

"Beautiful," he says. "Come look in the mirror."

I do, and it looks like a noose.

"You don't like it?" he asks. His smile dimming.

"No, *mi amor*. I do. I love it," I assure him. I can see he doesn't believe me.

He rips the clasp from around my throat.

I gasp, wait for the blow, not cringing this time.

Holding the necklace, he stares at me in the mirror, my pale face, my eyes with the fire of Venezuela, and the indent on my throat from the too-tight noose that he's given me.

Spinning on his heel, he retreats.

Without thinking, I follow.

He stands at the top of the stairs, frozen, his eyes fastened on the softly glowing gold in his hand. Perhaps he is thinking about returning to our bedroom? Doing what he's done so many times before?

He doesn't hear me, doesn't even know I'm there.

A simple shove is all it takes. Robert tumbles down the unforgiving steps, picks up speed. He hits the landing with a crunch. His neck at an impossible angle.

✗　✗　✗　✗

A young, good looking police officer talks with me in the sitting room. The paramedics have come and gone, and I'm tired of answering everyone's questions. My eyes are wet, the tears unable to stop. I readjust my grandmother's scarf, glad for its concealment.

"So you were in the library," he points to the adjoining room, "when you heard your husband fall down the steps?" He's asked me this question many times already.

"*Sì*," I say, my voice shaky. "I was getting ready to leave for a study session with some friends." I hold up my textbook, thick with page markers.

He asks for Jamal and Anne's names again. Asks which coffee shop.

I answer all his questions, my eyes streaming.

"And the necklace found next to him?"

I cry harder. "Our anniversary is… would be in two days's time. We were married two years ago on Columbus Day. Robert must have wanted to surprise me."

Finally, he closes his notebook, then asks, "What are you studying, Mrs. Carson?"

At this, I smile. "Christopher Columbus," I tell him. "But soon we start Simon Bolivar."

His forehead creases. "Who's that?"

"The *libertador* of Hispanic America from the Spanish Empire." I flip my book open to a page I recently bookmarked. I read, "The freedom of the New World is the hope of the Universe."

And this I now know is true.

The author wishes to acknowledge J.M. Cohen who translated Columbus's log-book, letters, and dispatches. For those interested in reading more of his logs, please see Cohen's, The Four Voyages of Christopher Columbus, *published by Penguin Press, 1969.*

Meg Opperman, a cultural anthropologist by training, has mastered the art of eavesdropping in bars around the globe in search of a story. She's had short stories published in both *EQMM* and *SHMM*, and writes a column (Write Side Up) for the *Washington Independent Review of Books*.

LUCKY MAN

by Steven Shrott

The cerulean blue crystal around my neck swayed back and forth as I shoved the knife into Thomas Semples, my business partner. We managed our New Age Shop, 'Good Fortunes,' for six years with great success. But when Thomas began embezzling, I decided that he should be off the payroll, so to speak.

As I drove home, I realized I was on quite a roll. Thomas had been my seventh murder in the last few weeks, and they had all gone exceptionally well. The police had no idea that I, Ronald Darling, committed these devastating (but amusing) acts.

I was a tad concerned as I hadn't received my full eight hours of sleep of late, what with so many requests for my talk: 'Crystals, from Egyptian to Aztec.' I have to admit I was dead tired.

When I think back on the murders thus far, I realized I'd made some amateur blunders—walking through blood, not wearing gloves, forgetting to wipe down surfaces I'd touched.

Some would say it must be some kind of miracle that I hadn't been caught. And they would be right. That miracle was my crystal.

It had come from the Hunto Sero Factory in Jakarta. Amethyst, clear as a water droplet. Of all the crystals I ever purchased, this was the most potent. From the moment I wrapped it around my neck, good luck surrounded my every action.

Of course, I did learn a lesson as well. I should ensure I have enough slumber before I murder anyone.

I left Semples's gaudy apartment and drove home, exhausted. I set the alarm for eight a.m. and awoke in the morning feeling wonderfully refreshed.

When I reached my store, I opened the glass door and marched in, as I supposed a commander might on the way to inspecting his troops. I began dusting, making everything clean and sparkly.

I waited for the onslaught of customers. But as it turned out, no onslaught today, just some badly dressed boors and tight-wad tourists.

At eleven, however, one of my favorite clients, Miss Delores Montgomery, trounced in. She's an older matron with a generous bosom. She gave me a toothy smile, then pointed toward a pink crystal resting on my wall shelf.

I delicately removed the item and laid it onto my red velvet show-pad. "This would really bring out your eyes, Miss Montgomery."

She blushed. "It's beautiful." She scooped it up and held it against her chest.

"Do you feel the energy?"

"Yes. How much?"

"A very reasonable eighty-two fifty."

Her face fell and she placed the crystal back onto my show pad. "That's a little too dear for me, Mr. Darling."

"I understand. But you see crystals that emanate such powerful vibrations are rare. This is the first I've found in over three years."

She smiled, and then I saw it—-the glint in her eye that told me the sale was mine. However, when she searched her purse, I sensed something wrong.

"Mr. Darling, I have to be honest, I only have sixty dollars and that's food shopping money for myself and my elderly father."

"You're a good customer, Miss Montgomery. You can pay me the rest next time." I winked at her and opened up my hand. She draped the money over it.

Miss Montgomery left with a lilt and I was pleased I could bring a little sunshine into an older lady's dreary existence.

Of course that evening, I did exactly the opposite. My victim was Aaron Bevins, a banker at City Wide Investments. I had asked him for a loan of twenty grand to enlarge my shop. However, he was too obtuse to recognize a lucrative business opportunity.

I must say last night's sleep had done me a world of good and I believe my actions were error-free this evening. Of course when you had the power of the crystal working through you—no worries. I left Bevins, his expensive Indian carpet soaking up all the blood.

The next afternoon, I headed off to a lunch date at Chez Panisse with my new sweetheart Catherine Halterton. I met her about six weeks ago—the crystal strikes again. She had this ethereal beauty. Bouncy blond hair, delicious creamy complexion, tight little body.

When I arrived, I immediately noticed her sitting at our table, face drawn. Perhaps something to do with the recent loss of her job.

"Hello, buttercup." I kissed her sensuous lips.

"Hi, Ronald."

We ate while she filled me in on her job search struggles.

"I just keep hitting a brick wall. In the computer programming industry it's all contacts and none of mine seem to be able to help much. I do have an interview later today, but I don't give it much hope." She began weeping.

I was a sucker for tears and knew I had to assist her. "Catherine, I know you don't believe in such things, but I'd be willing to lend you my crystal to get you through this crisis. It has been very lucky for me." I removed it from my neck and placed it into her delicate hands.

I immediately noticed a change in her demeanour. Brighter, happier.

"I really don't think it could do…"

I turned my palms up. "Can it hurt to try?"

She nodded half-heartedly.

"I only ask one thing, my dear. You will most likely see results today, so if you could return it by this evening, that would be heavenly. I have something where I also need good fortune to smile on me."

"Absolutely. I'll call you around seven."

We ended our lunch with a lovely tiramisu and a juicy kiss.

That night, I sat in my apartment waiting for her call. I was certainly interested to see the effect the crystal would have on her employment difficulties, but I also needed it before the next of my nightly excursions. I planned to teach a lesson to some pisser who called me a 'dandy' at the Kingsmill Tavern up the street. I dare say his vocal cords would soon find it difficult to pronounce that word or any other, for that matter. I grinned at the thought.

While waiting, I watched TV. *Dexter* was on. It gave me some deliciously creative ideas that I could incorporate into my current routine.

The clock struck seven-thirty and I still hadn't received any communication from Catherine. It concerned me greatly, so I decided to call her. No answer. I didn't like the sound of that.

I tried again at eight, nothing. Nine, ten, eleven. Where was she? More importantly, where was my crystal?

Eventually, I fell asleep on my couch and by the time I had awoken, morning had arrived. I felt rested, but still upset. I drove to Catherine's apartment and banged on the door. She answered after a bit, wearing the lavender silk robe I purchased for her birthday.

I tried to calm myself, spoke in my soft voice. "I don't mean to bother you honey, but I was worried. You said you'd call."

"Oh, right," she said, looking dazed. "Some things came up and I guess I forgot. I'm sorry."

"So how did the interview go?"

"Great. The boss took one look at my resumé and I got the job, almost like magic."

"Do you believe in the power of the crystals now?"

"Well, sure it could have been that. But I do have a strong resumé and they needed someone right away."

I guess a practical person like her would never understand. Oh, well, I tried.

Suddenly a strange look appeared on her face. "Listen, I'm in the middle of something here. Could we talk later?"

"Sure, sure. I'd just like to get the crystal back."

"Oh, uh... the crystal. Look, why don't we meet for lunch at Roberto's and I'll give it to you then."

"I suppose that would be…"

The door shut.

The morning at my shop seemed to go on forever. I was too tense to be my usual engaging self and though I had a few customers, I wasn't able to make a sale.

At twelve, I high-tailed it over to Roberto's. Catherine sat at a table in the back and I joined her.

We small-talked for a bit. She loved her first day on the job and everything seemed to go well. I did sense her being a little distant toward me, but chalked it up to new-job-stress. In the back of my mind, I worried that something happened to the crystal. However, when I asked for it, she instantly produced it from her bag. My whole body relaxed as I put it on. I felt as if I could do no wrong.

"Perhaps we can get together tonight for dinner?" I asked.

"Sorry, they want me to work late."

"Already?"

"What can I do? I'm new."

I nodded, in the way an understanding boyfriend would nod, then kissed her goodbye—not letting her know I was aware she met someone new.

The clues were all there. The morning where she wanted to get rid of me, the distant attitude at lunch, the sudden overtime. But actually, I didn't feel anything bad toward her. There were other fishes in the sea of life.

No, I directed my rage at the scoundrel who had taken her from me. I was a hundred percent sure he knew she had a lover. These jackasses always do. And they steal them away just for sport. I would discover his name and give him a taste of my special brand of medicine.

That night I followed Catherine to a house in one of the better neighborhoods. I suppose she was trading up.

I waited outside, patiently, giving them time to reconnect before I surprised them, possibly, *in flagrante*.

As I studied the house, I wondered how I would enter, but my crystal must have been on the job as I found an open window on the side. I climbed in, moved swiftly down the stairs and located the bedroom. The slightly ajar door enabled me to see Catherine lying on the bed asleep.

I removed my gun. Normally, I used a knife for my dirty deeds, but I believe that stealing another man's woman is the lowest act of a despicable coward, so I decided a pistol was in order. I squeezed through the space of the open door, about to aim the gun. Suddenly, Catherine awoke, horrified.

I was surprised. After all, I had so much good luck thus far. Having her awake could be awkward.

"Ronald, what are you doing?"

"This is none of your business. This is between this usurper, this blasphemer, and me."

A sad smile filled her lips. "I should have told you. I'm sorry. On the same day I got the new job, I also found someone new. We just clicked. I can't believe how lucky I am."

Maybe she was lucky, but her partner soon wouldn't be.

I fired six quick shots into the jumble of blankets beside Catherine, being careful not to hit a single hair on her lovely head. I guess in some ways I still cared for her.

Suddenly, I heard a voice. "Were you aiming that at me?"

I turned to find her man holding a gun and wearing a policeman outfit. Apparently, he hadn't been in the bed as I'd thought.

I tugged at my crystal, hoping to get my mojo back. But the cord broke and it dropped to the ground, shattering. I felt horrible, but I couldn't think about that now.

"That is attempted murder, my friend."

I tried the sympathy approach. "Officer, who wouldn't be upset by another man sleeping with his girlfriend? It's only natural—it brings out one's basest emotions."

"Is that what happened when you killed Thomas Semples?"

"Not sure what you're referring to."

"Cut the act. Semples came to us a week ago. He had cameras placed all over his apartment, desperately worried about being killed by his business partner. We have video of you sticking a knife in him, as well as fingerprints. We were all set to lock you up for life, but strangely the tape, somehow, got erased and the fingerprints disappeared. We lost all the evidence. Never seen anything like it."

The crystals had worked their magic. I needed to get that magic back. I reached down, scooped up the pieces on the ground, stood up. I stared at the crystals for a moment, enjoying the way the light refracted off them, then held them against my heart.

Everything was going to be fine.

My eyes shifted to the officer, now sure of myself, defiant even. "I don't know what you're talking about."

At that moment, I noticed Catherine wearing a crystal just like mine. "Where did you get that?"

She blushed. "Well, see after I got the job and met Dan on the same day…" She glided over to the officer, put her arm around his shoulder, "…I figured maybe this stuff does work. I didn't really want to part with it. I didn't have the money to buy you another crystal, they're expensive. So I found one that looked the same at Solly's Discount Emporium."

"Discount Emporium?" My mouth fell open as I dropped the trash that sullied my hands to the ground.

I was arrested, of course, and my string of bad luck continued. They connected me to all of the murders I'd done and a few I hadn't. Then I got sent to death row where I suffered a broken leg, due to a misunderstanding with one of the guards.

Bad things happen to me on a daily basis now. It's horrendous. But things will get better soon. I just figured out how to use the prison phone to make a long distance call to a certain factory in Jakarta.

Steve Shrott's short stories have appeared in ten anthologies as well as numerous online and print magazines. He has written two humorous mystery novels (*Audition for Death* and *Dead Men Don't Get Married*,) and a "how-to book" on comedy-writing. Some of his jokes are in the Smithsonian Institution.

ONE HEADLIGHT

by Steve Liskow

Homicide detective Richmond Flood watched the technicians finish dusting for latents and upload their pictures into a laptop while the EMTs bagged the body. Blaire Trieste, the manager of Queen Anne's Lace, the lingerie boutique in the mall, died in front of her desk, still fully clothed except for her shoes. One red stiletto lay under the desk and the other lay in an evidence bag. Contusions on the dead woman's face seemed to match the blood-streaked heel.

The tech showed Flood the bag. "Boy, talk about being pumped, huh?" His glasses made him resemble Harry Potter's evil twin.

"Give me a break, Ronnie."

The air in the boutique smelled pink, matching the negligees, corsets, and other weapons of mass seduction on display. Flood decided it was supposed to be sexy. It also made his sinuses feel like a toothpaste tube being squeezed in the middle and gave his eyes the sandpaper itch he associated with ragweed season.

The woman standing just outside the office door had red eyes, too, but she was still crying. Even in heels, Clara Bowie barely reached Flood's chin. She wore an aquamarine silk blouse and black leather skirt that gave off the same vibe as the underdressed mannequins.

"God, I still can't believe it." Clara's ID badge bounced when she blew her nose again. Below her ID, she wore the pink ribbon pin for breast cancer awareness. Flood kept his eyes on the woman so she didn't think he was checking out the red satin bra and thong on the torso to his left. A whole platoon wearing different colors stood behind it. Two uniformed officers stood outside the still-lowered grille at the entrance arch, holding back the crowd trying to see through those shimmery silver torsos. The shop usually opened at noon on Sunday, but Clara found Blaire Trieste at ten and called the police.

"When I left last night, she and Marina were tying up loose ends for the show. And now she's…"

"Show?" Flood fought back a sneeze. The perfumed sachets on the table behind him attacked his sinuses like ants at a picnic. Ronnie the Tech slid by him to fingerprint the other clerks for comparison later. Jerry Riggins, Flood's partner, talked to a clerk with hair the color of a new penny, lipstick and nails to match. Another woman with a silver pageboy stood next to her and they nodded in unison. Penny and Nicole, Flood remembered. The Coyne sisters.

"The fund-raiser downstairs," Clara said. "You passed it in the center court."

Flood looked through the grille again. Sure enough, he saw people checking speakers and lights below them. "Where's the money going?"

"Breast cancer research."

Which explained everybody's pink pin. Now Flood remembered reading about it in that morning's *Courant*. Queen Anne's Lace was supplying the lingerie for models to display, Tress For Success on the lower level was doing hair and make-up, CPTV was broadcasting the whole show, and members of the UConn women's basketball team and the WNBA's Connecticut Sun were signing autographs. Even with Flood's limited grasp of public relations, he thought someone had come up with a slam dunk.

"Ms. Bowie," he said. "Was Ms. Trieste wearing the same clothes when you left last night?"

Clara's eyes flickered toward the office again. "Uh-huh. With that flesh-colored cami, it looked like she wasn't wearing anything under her blazer. Black slacks, and scarlet Manolos to match the jacket."

Dressed to kill. Flood caught himself before he said it out loud. At the register, Ronnie fingerprinted the Asian woman wearing a shimmery purple blouse that matched her fingernails. Or vice versa. Her face looked impassive, but her eyes showed that she was working at it.

"What time did you leave last night?"

"Nine. I offered to stay, but Blaire said they were almost done so I let myself out the back…"

"Can you think of anyone who would want to kill her?"

"Oh, God, everyone loved Blaire. Even with business down, she was trying to keep Marina on."

"Marina?"

"Marina Santini. She's only been here eight or nine months, but she's amazing." Clara took another tissue. "Blaire let Corporate think the fund-raiser was her idea, but Marina's done like ninety-nine per cent of the work."

"Really." Flood felt that third cup of coffee. He knew the public restroom was down the escalator and beyond the center court.

Clara reached for another tissue. "She found the models—don't ask me where—she persuaded the teams to have players come in to do the signing, I think she even talked CPTV into the live coverage."

The uniformed officers raised the grille so the EMTs could roll the gurney through. The crowd seemed to pull back and surge forward at the same time. Everyone wanted to see the body bag but no one wanted to get too close, just in case it was contagious.

"Thank you, Ms. Bowie." Flood let the woman stumble over to the Asian clerk in purple, who hugged her. Ronnie the Tech stalked Penny and Nicole. Jerry Riggins left them at his mercy and approached Flood.

"The ME says the woman's been dead twelve to fifteen hours." His words smelled of breath mints and the knot in his tie looked as perfect as his teeth. If his eyes weren't so close together, he could be a game show host.

Flood's watch said twelve-ten. "The store closed at nine and the grille was down, so whoever killed her came in the employee's entrance. Or was already here."

"Yeah." Jerry held a pair of turquoise panties in front of his face and Flood could still distinguish his features through them. "That means the babe you just talked to, the Asian chick, and the blonde over there with the clipboard."

The Asian woman tried not to stare at them. Her hands couldn't stay still.

Jerry twirled the panties on his finger and his grin resembled a Cadillac grille. "Man, I'd like to see that babe with the silver hair in these. Or maybe out of them."

"You're the world's biggest horn dog, Jerry."

"It's true." Jerry replaced the panties with the same reverence he might have shown the Shroud of Turin. "It's a hell of a burden, but I do my best to live up to it."

Flood returned to Blaire Trieste's office, where the air was less perfumed so he could actually breathe. A chalk outline showed where the woman had fallen, the corner of the desk sticky where she must have struck her head. Flood looked through the desk drawers but nothing seemed out of place.

The pilot light on the PC monitor glowed pale orange. Flood tapped the space bar and watched Blaire Trieste's desktop materialize. He clicked the blinking icon at the lower left—

"Your last browsing session closed unexpectedly"—and found himself staring at a Facebook page. Blaire's cover shot was close-up and personal of a woman wearing a red thong that revealed a delicate butterfly tattoo on the left buttocks. The butterfly's wings matched the thong—and the dead woman's jacket and shoes.

She had a dozen fresh messages and he jotted down the senders's names: Ben82, Jack the Knife, HardRide. They all discussed hooking up, past, present, or future. Social media, indeed. He wondered if Blaire Trieste had a steady boyfriend or a steady stream of them. Her status was "Single" and she was interested in "men."

He scrolled her list of friends and recognized the Coyne sisters in what looked like apparel from the store and Clara Bowie with a beach shot as her cover. Clara's status claimed she was married to Jack. Marina Santini appeared, too. Her cover shot was the pink breast cancer awareness pin.

Flood clicked the "Home" icon and found an email that kept TrystAndShout logged in to a Hotmail account. He saw thirty more messages, mostly discussing her social life again, and with a few of the same names. He made a note to have forensics check out the PC.

Her documents listed a "Marina Rec." Clara Bowie was right: Marina Santini was leaving Queen Anne's Lace in another two weeks. Blaire made a point of saying it was because they were downsizing, and praised her humor, creativity, and ability to work with others. One paragraph even told about how she found the models for the fund-raiser.

When Flood stepped out of the office again, Jerry was talking to the Asian woman. Clara Bowie fiddled with an iPod that was apparently the store's music system, preparing to open the boutique a half-hour late. The Coyne sisters were arranging negligees near the display windows. Nicole watched Jerry hitting on the Asian woman.

"We called her 'Blaire Tryst' as a joke." The woman's name tag called her "June Smith," and Flood wondered if that was a joke, too. "Blaire was very… popular."

"Lots of boyfriends, huh? Anyone special?"

"Not that I am aware of. But she may well have had an assignation planned for last night."

Flood watched Jerry grapple with "Assignation" and refused to define it for him.

"Excuse me," he said. "Ms. Smith, do you know if she had problems with any of these men? A fight, any threats?"

"It is possible. Blaire was sometimes… impulsive."

"What do you mean by that?" Jerry asked.

The woman looked toward the crowd beyond the grille. "I should not speak ill of the dead without firsthand knowledge."

She walked over to rearrange the panties Jerry examined. His eyes checked out her leather slacks, three shades darker than her blouse, and he oozed over next to her again.

Flood approached the blond woman who juggled a clipboard and a cell phone. When she looked up so he could see her face, he felt himself break stride.

Marina Santini had shoulder-length waves two shades darker than butter and blue eyes round enough to roll down her perfect nose. Those eyes seemed to see headlights approaching much too quickly.

"Ms. Santini, I'm Detective Flood. I'm sorry to bother you right now, but I need to ask you a few questions."

"Of course." Her voice felt like butterscotch syrup, but she seemed to be reminding herself how to talk.

"What time did you leave here last night?"

"A little after nine. Maybe nine-fifteen. I don't remember exactly." She wore a charcoal blazer over a blouse with a pink stripe that matched the breast cancer pin on her lapel.

"Was anyone else still here? Besides Ms. Trieste?"

"No. June and Clara left a few minutes before I did. We'd locked up in front and made sure everyone had picked up their ensembles for today, and she said she was leaving in a few minutes, too."

"Ensembles?"

"For the fashion show downstairs. Bust Breast Cancer. We donated the lingerie, and CPTV is going to auction everything off after the women model it."

"How'd you come up with the name 'Bust Breast Cancer?'" Jerry spoke before Flood even smelled his breath mints.

In heels, Marina Santini was Flood's five-eleven. "I wanted to call it 'Tits And Assets,' but Blaire almost had a seizure."

"I like it," Flood said.

"How about 'Bucks For Boobs?'" She arched her eyebrows at Jerry.

Flood shook his head before Jerry could answer. "Someone might think it's for politicians."

"You guys just like talking about breasts, right?" Marina Santini caught Flood looking at her finger, the one without a ring. At the center court, someone was teaching the PA system to squeal. June Smith approached Jerry again.

"Detective Riggins, may I show you something for your OAO?" Her voice sounded like she could spread it on a muffin.

"'OAO?'" Jerry didn't quite smack his lips.

"One and Only." She led him to a display of robes and Flood turned back to Marina Santini, who rolled those amazing blue eyes.

"We've got a zillion jokes here." Her face stayed slightly less serious than cramps. "Most of them old as the hills, if you'll excuse the expression."

"Really." Flood watched the uniforms raise the grille and customers drift into the store. Soft music came up on the iPod.

"Yeah," Marina said. "About once a day I hear June say, 'Sir, could I interest you in a sheer teddy?'"

Her eyes stared into Flood's. "Do you have any idea who might have…?"

"It's either someone from work or someone she knew." Flood saw two UConn warm-up jackets appear below. That damned perfume was attacking his sinuses again.

"Ms. Trieste was letting you go in two weeks."

"I know. We need to cut back, and I was the last hire." Her eyes looked three times as old as the rest of her. "That means I'm a suspect, doesn't it?"

"I'm afraid so."

"Some days you wonder if it's even worth gnawing through the restraints." The woman bit her lip. "Oh, God, that's one of Blaire's lines."

"Really," Flood said again.

"She said she was going to write me a good recommendation."

"She did." Flood watched the woman struggle to breathe normally. "She gave you credit for the fund-raiser idea and finding the models." He couldn't take his eyes off her face. "And you were in a perfect position to persuade them, weren't you?"

She looked toward the register, where Clara Bowie wrapped three thongs for a girl who looked barely old enough to drive.

"Were you one of the ones who called your boss 'Blaire Tryst?'"

"We all did. Blaire thought it was funny. At least, she acted like she did."

"Well, her Hotmail address is 'TrystAndShout.'" Flood kept his voice neutral. "Do you know if she was meeting anyone last night?"

"Blaire spend Saturday night alone? Maybe when the moon falls into Long Island Sound. But that doesn't mean she had anything lined up yet." Marina seemed to hear herself. "That sounds catty, doesn't it?"

"Just a little, yeah."

In the corridor outside, a young girl in purple Barney overalls screamed that she wanted a Big Cookie, and her mom screamed back that she'd just had lunch and the line was too long anyway.

"I used to feel jealous about her. So beautiful, men willing to crawl naked over broken glass to be with her..."

"You're very attractive, too, Ms. Santini."

Her eyes retreated. "Thank you."

"Did the technician fingerprint you so we can compare your prints to the ones in Ms. Trieste's office?"

"Yes, but you'll find dozens from all of us. We're in and out a hundred times a day."

Clara Bowie bagged a bra and panty set that made spider webs look like hawsers. David Bowie's "Suffragette City" pumped through the store.

"You pointed out that last night was Saturday night. So you didn't have a date, either?"

"I'm still kind of dealing with…" She bit her lip. "My fiancé dumped me."

"I'm sorry." Flood watched the woman watch June Smith flirt with Jerry. "Does that have anything to do with why you put this show together?"

"I suppose that was a lot of it. I needed to convince myself…"

"Sure." Flood decided Marina Santini was better off without an idiot for a husband.

She fired off the statistics about how many women were diagnosed every day (not quite 500), how many died (one every ten minutes), how many could have been saved if they'd had a check-up. Her mind seemed to be on the stage, the store, and Flood simultaneously.

"If early detection is so important, why don't more women get check-ups?" he asked.

"Why do so many teenagers die in traffic accidents?" A silver bracelet peeked from under her left cuff. "When you're young, you think you'll live forever. We think of cancer as an old person's disease. I used to, anyway."

"Me too," Flood said. "How old are your models for this show?"

"The oldest is forty-six, the youngest is twenty-nine. None of them are professionals, but all of them are breast cancer survivors."

"You found them through the hospital's cancer site, didn't you?"

Her chin rose slightly. "We started our own group, chatted a lot. It gave me the idea, and a bunch of them offered to help before I even pitched it to Blaire." She put down her clipboard. "You wouldn't know about that Web site unless you have cancer, too."

He let out the breath he didn't know he was holding and reminded himself that she was still a suspect, just like June Smith and Clara Bowie.

"I'm thirty-two, and my PSA is 7.8." He realized he was whispering. "I go in for a prostatectomy in three weeks."

"It's very scary, isn't it? Like for no reason God has decided you pissed Him off." She winced. "Sorry, bad choice of words."

"I'll bet your fiancé said worse, didn't he?"

Jerry handed June Smith his card. When she slid it into her blouse, his eyes almost rolled out of his head.

The music changed to some female singer. Marina licked her lips and Flood envied her tongue.

"I'm guessing a lot of the other women had the same kind of thing happen, too, didn't they? That's why they were so willing to help you out on this."

Marina's eyes looked the way Joan of Arc's might have when she watched the flames nibbling at her feet. "They're doing something for a cause, but they're making a statement for themselves, too. They had cancer and they survived. They're alive, they're healthy… and they're still desirable women."

Her voice faded and Flood felt like a bully.

"Look." Her hand felt cold when he took it and turned her toward the center court. "Lots of people are gathering and the show doesn't even start for half an hour."

"Oh, God," she said. "Half an hour? I have to get my stuff."

She stepped behind the counter and made eye contact with Clara Bowie before she picked up a leather gym bag. June Smith came over and hugged her, the girls with metallic hair only steps behind.

"Break a leg, Marina."

"Thanks, Clarie."

"You will knock them dead, Girlfriend." June gave "girl" and "friend" equal stress.

Flood followed Marina Santini through the arch. Behind him, he heard June tell Jerry that the others had been giving her a pep talk for weeks. She stressed both "pep" and "talk," too.

Below them, the center court looked like the Grand Canyon done in faux marble, the colorful crowd milling like jelly beans. The electronic marquee blinked "BUST BREAST CANCER, SUN 1:00." Along the far rail, spectators obscured Eddie Bauer, Liz Claiborne, and the Sprint Store. Marina's gaze was frozen but Flood heard her chanting.

"I think I can, I think I can, I think I can."

"How much do you expect to raise today?" He saw her take a deep breath and caught himself wondering about her body.

"We're aiming for a hundred thousand."

She ticked points off on her fingers. Her nail polish matched her ribbon pin, too. "We've got cheesecake and the survivors for the media coverage. The players's autographs are five dollars each. CPTV is taking pledges for us, and Dave Rabideau is emceeing the auction for all the outfits. That will run all through Breast Cancer Awareness Week."

As they rode down the escalator, her voice picked up speed. "Khandy Tarte from local access is here, too. Do you believe that's her real name? I don't. Why didn't she change it?"

"Or become a stripper?" Flood said. "Then she could buy all her stuff from you, couldn't she? Get a professional discount?"

"No." Marina's pink nails seemed to dig into the handrail. "The strippers buy their gear in Hartford. Our stuff isn't break-away and we don't carry much latex."

"Marina, breathe." Flood thought that if he ran his hand up her back, she'd thrum like a harp. "Let me finish upstairs, then I'll come back here. Maybe we can do coffee or something? I understand that your fiancé's dumping you takes some time to get over, so I won't—"

Her eyes filled up. "At least he waited until I came out of surgery."

"In the hospital?" Flood felt ashamed for his gender. "He really is an idiot. And slime."

"No." Her eyes reminded him of a little girl facing a huge barking dog. "What kind of asshole would buy a car with a missing headlight?"

"A Mercedes?" He suspected that she was quoting her Gone and Only. "A Rolls? Hell yes, any day of the week."

Dave Rabideau studied a clipboard, Khandy Tarte reading over his shoulder. He looked casual, she looked like a bad heavy metal video. David Bowie was still hovering in the back of Flood's mind and he knew he had to look at the dead woman's computer again.

He returned to Queen Anne's Lace, where June Smith and the Coynes flowed among the customers and Clara Bowie rang up sales. Jerry meandered through the mannequins and beamed like he'd found the Holy Grail. Flood went into the office and opened Blaire Trieste's pictures. The cheeky shot from her Facebook cover winked back at him. He clicked on the picture and found a series of numbers long enough to fit on a freight train. Sure, Blaire couldn't have held the camera herself to get that angle. He went back into her Facebook account and found the posting when she'd changed her cover shot. Forty people liked it, including Jack the Knife.

Flood returned to the showroom.

When the customers drifted toward the center court to watch the show, he approached Clara Bowie.

"Ms. Bowie, does the store have a drop box for the receipts?"

"Right here." She nodded below the register. "And a small safe in the office."

"Do you know the combination?"

"None of us do. I don't know if Blaire has it written down anywhere. Why? Do you think someone was trying to rob us and she caught him?"

"'Him?'"

"Well, I assumed a man, since he beat Blaire to death." Only the cops and the clerks were still in the store, clustered in the entrance arch to hear the echoing PA downstairs. The iPod changed to another female singer Flood didn't recognize. He stared at Clara.

"That's odd because you, Ms. Santini, and Ms. Smith were the three people who had access. Remember, the grille was down and locked. You said so yourself."

"Um, right."

"Why don't we step into the office?" Flood caught Jerry's eye and motioned him to follow.

He sat at the desk and brought up the letter of recommendation for Marina Santini again.

"Didn't you tell me that Ms. Trieste took credit for this fundraiser herself?"

"Um, I thought so. She said something a few days ago that…"

"No, this letter says Marina Santini put the whole thing together. Getting the TV coverage, finding the athletes for autographs…" He watched Clara hover on the side of the desk away from the chalk outline. "And you all encouraged her to be in the show, too, didn't you?"

"Totally. I mean, she's really pretty, and she doesn't have any self-confidence after, well… I guess you know that from reading the letter, don't you?"

"Her fiancé broke off their engagement after she had a mastectomy."

"Men really are bastards sometimes, aren't they?"

"We are," he agreed. "But deep down, Ms. Santini still believes he may have done the right thing."

"What crap. Excuse my language."

"You, on the other hand, are a healthy and attractive woman." Flood saw Jerry register where he was going. "So when your husband started running around, you had every right to be angry."

"Excuse me?" Clara Bowie's eyes seemed to bounce.

"Ms. Trieste's Facebook was open on the PC, dozens of messages from men. A couple of them more than once. And one of them is Jack the Knife. He took the picture on her desktop. A fairly intimate portrait, wouldn't you say?"

Clara's face turned that same shade of porcelain he remembered from an hour earlier.

"Jack as in Bowie, right? Your husband."

"That's the craziest thing I've ever heard."

"It gets crazier," Flood said. "Blaire Trieste is about eight inches taller than you are, Marina Santini is a good six inches, and so is June Smith. Either of them would have hit her in the forehead or temple. But you could only reach her cheeks and chin with her shoe. She hit her head when she fell, didn't she?"

Clara Bowie's face faded from porcelain to avocado green.

Jerry and the uniforms escorted her out, Jerry waving to June Smith on the way.

Flood returned to the top of the escalator and watched twenty lovely women strut their stuff below him. Their costumes weren't transparent, but they were still daring enough to flirt with local zoning laws. They never made a second of it look cheap, though, and Flood wondered if he would be as brave if he were in their place.

The loveliest of them all had shoulder-length hair two shades darker than butter and blue eyes he could see even from the upper level. She wore a corset with a strategic ruffle at the top, and he wondered how many of the other women had lost a breast, too. He eased down the escalator in time to watch Marina Santini make her last turn on the runway.

A guy in the crowd called out to her, "Hey, baby, what's your sign?"

She never broke stride.

"Cancer, Dude. What's yours?"

Make that a zillion and one jokes.

Twenty minutes later, she emerged from the dressing room talking with two other women, all three of them glowing. She hugged them before she joined Flood and her eyes turned older again.

"We've made an arrest." He watched the tension drain out of her body. They approached Higher Grounds, near Lord and Taylor, and her pace slowed.

"Are you sure coffee's a good idea in your condition?"

"I can live with Plan B. What's your comfort food of choice?"

"Maybe ice cream?"

"Cone, sundae, you name it."

"Sundae."

The corner of her mouth twitched.

"Two scoops?"

A zillion and two jokes.

✗

Steve Liskow (www.steveliskow.com) is a former actor, theatrical director and English teacher whose short stories have earned an Edgar nomination and the Black Orchid Novella Award. Many of his novels take place in his home state of Connecticut and feature issues including teen trafficking and a shooting at a public school. *Blood on the Tracks* (2013) introduces Detroit PI Chris "Woody" Guthrie and draws on Steve's experience as a guitarist and DJ. The book won Honorable Mention for the Writer's Digest Self-Published Novel Awards in 2014.

THE HOLMES IMPERSONATOR

by Janice Law

Yes, that's me in full Sherlock mode, complete with deerstalker hat and my long gray cloak—don't call it a coat! Lightweight wool, thank goodness, but still warm on summer days when I am out greeting tour and camp buses and Holmesian *aficionados*. One thing I've learned about the great man is that it must always have been chilly on Baker Street.

Actually, I've learned more about Mr. Holmes than I ever intended. Back in drama school, I'd done Shaw and Shakespeare; Kushner and Albee. I had, make that, I have, ambitions. The last thing I'd figured on was working as a living billboard, exchanging *bon mots* drawn from the Master of Detection.

No, indeed. But after a little avant-garde theatre company went belly up, a summer stock job failed to come through and a TV pilot sank without a trace, I needed cash and, maybe even more, the chance to dress up and be someone else on a regular basis. Hence my tenure at the Sherlock Holmes Museum, a somewhat eccentric outfit with an excellent library and a fine display of prints and memorabilia, plus special exhibitions dealing with crime and detection. Our latest, *From Holmes to CSI*, has proved very popular.

As have I. I was hired for a few weeks one summer as a sort of glorified parking attendant and tour guide. Well, whatever the part, however small the role, prepare, prepare, prepare, as my old drama prof used to say. I started reading the famous *Strand* stories during my lunch hour and making notes of particularly pithy phrases on my iPhone.

Pretty soon, I was exchanging opinions on Irene Adler with besotted visitors and debating the finer points of *The Adventure of Silver Blaze* or *The Copper Beeches*. Adults were easy to please. Throw out one of Holmes's pet phrases like, "My method is founded upon the observation of trifles," pretend to puff on my big carved pipe, and they were satisfied.

Kids, now, are a tougher audience. But it wasn't long before I understood the great detective's system, a mix of careful observation, relevant information, and logic. Although I initially believed that I had the first and third in the bag, my first few attempts at Holmesian deduction showed that observation needed to be kicked up a notch.

Relevant information was a little harder, but fortunately our tour group schedule was a big help and the internet replaced Holmes's capacious memory. Soon I was able not only to greet the campers from Camp Kik-a-Nap-Ou or the local elementary but to ask how they liked beginning canoeing (an easy one, bandaged fingers and blisters everywhere) or to pick out the survivors of the annual Field Day (sunburns galore and little pins for the victors).

Of course, I had to be careful. As I worked my way into the character, I sometimes noticed things that I wished I hadn't: the child with the black eye and bruises on her legs. The couple clearly at odds, the old man uneasy with his younger attendant. My Sherlock's investigative brief definitely had its limitations.

To avoid problems, I came up with the idea of staging little crime scenes (mostly cribbed from the original stories) and letting the visitors "play Sherlock Holmes." My Watson—I haven't yet mentioned Dr. Jean Watson, PhD., museum director and another ambitious soul—approved a trial. Between us, we came up with a scene in one of the exhibition spaces, laid clues about, and gave the visitors a synopsis of the problem.

Eventually these Test Your Skills problems secured my part time post, which with a little bartending and the occasional acting gig, kept me afloat. The museum was good about giving me time off for auditions, and I began to rely on my job there.

So I had an interest in the Sherlock Holmes Museum's erratic finances, and when one of our board members offered to do a holiday benefit, I was more than willing to don my tweeds and deerstalker. I love an audience in any case. Not so My Watson, who was as nervous as a cat the whole week before, anxious that all should go well and apprehensive about what I assured her would be a marvelous improvisational opportunity.

To keep her happy, I agreed to use a scripted problem—if something more suitable didn't turn up.

"Let's hope it won't," she said.

"The party will go well, Jean. You've done a terrific job with the museum."

"But this is so important for our future. We all need to be at our very best."

"Sherlock Holmes will be at the top of his game," I promised.

On the evening of the benefit, I even smoked a pipe before setting out, so that I came with the right smoky aroma. And from the moment we stepped into the big, two-story hallway, I was super alert and ready to notice whatever could be turned to entertainment and surprise.

There was a lot to see. Paul and Julia Bergman had an old stone-built mansion with the dormers and balustrades and slate roofs and handsome terraces that the McMansions try to duplicate. This was the real thing, complete with fine boxwood hedges and noble oaks without, and a small forest of conifers within.

The whole place smelled like the forest primeval. A twenty-foot spruce anchored the hallway, and massive wreaths hung over every fireplace. Herds of golden reindeer with jeweled collars frolicked amidst the greenery, while golden flights of angels with jeweled crowns soared above. With half a dozen different designs for each species, the whole effect was sumptuous.

That was just the entry. Through the double doors, we saw that the living room and dining room were similarly decorated.

"Oh, it's exquisite," said My Watson. "We're so grateful that you've opened your home for the museum."

"Our pleasure," Paul Bergman said. "Julia just loves the Christmas season. She's always decorated every room in the house, and since she discovered St. Armond's Design a couple of years ago—well, you can see the results." He gave a glance upstairs as he spoke, and you didn't have to be Sherlock to deduce that something important was keeping Julia Bergman from her guests. "Go ahead," Paul said, "and get yourselves drinks. I'll let Julia know you're here."

Although we'd arrived early, there were already friends and museum patrons admiring another massive blue spruce and giving orders to the barman. My Watson embarked on some serious schmoozing, and I made silent calculations about the cost of this decorating extravaganza, while keeping one eye on the foyer.

Suddenly there was a cry from upstairs and a door slamming. A moment later, Paul Bergman appeared beside My Watson. "Problem," he said and drew her into a little office off the foyer. Naturally, I followed.

"What has happened?" Jean asked. She was as white as a sheet, foreseeing the loss of funding, of various grant applications, of the invaluable favor of the Bergman family.

"Julia's diamonds—the LaFarge family's diamonds—are missing."

"And you've called the police?"

"I've called the Chief of Police," he said.

Sherlock nodded sagely. Nothing less than the top man for this outfit.

"But there's been a serious accident on I-95. Bus overturned. The chance of anyone getting here is very unlikely at the moment."

"I assume this is something very valuable," I said. My Watson gave me a look, but Paul nodded unhappily.

"The LaFarge necklace was designed over a hundred years ago by Tiffany. It has a dozen flawless diamonds set in platinum and a large sapphire pendant. One of a kind and very nearly priceless," he said. "Julia is quite distraught."

"As well she might be!" My Watson exclaimed. "Is there anything we can do?"

He shook his head. "I did want Julia to keep it quiet, but I'm afraid the guests already sense something's amiss. And if someone in the party—not that I think for a moment that one of our guests—but if someone here has the necklace, they will surely use the disruption as an excuse to leave."

"Not necessarily," I said.

My Watson went, if anything, a shade paler.

"You know we had planned a little detective diversion for the evening. Why not pretend the loss of the necklace was staged? Why not let Sherlock Holmes investigate for a bit? If nothing else, we will gain time for you and Mrs. Bergman to continue your search. Dr. Watson, who I think knows most of the guests, can keep a discreet eye out for anyone who leaves early."

Well, My Watson didn't much like this idea which certainly did smack of improvisation, but Paul Bergman was willing to do anything that would calm his wife. He went upstairs to speak to her, leaving Jean and me to look at the walls and avoid eye contact.

"We have a chance of a patrol officer at some time tonight," Paul said when he returned. "I really wonder why I pay my taxes."

"He—or she—will know the procedures," I said. It didn't seem the time to channel Sherlock's opinion of local constabulary.

"In the meantime, I think we'll try your idea." Paul stepped into the living room, got a glass from the barman, and tapped it for attention. He looked flushed and angry, but give him credit: this was a cool operator, and he launched into as smooth an introduction as any Sherlock could expect. "As you know," he began, "we're celebrating the Sherlock Holmes Museum here tonight, and the great man has agreed not only to put in an appearance, but to help us out with a little mystery."

Exclamations of pleasure and, I thought, relief. Julia Bergman's cry of dismay had carried even over the festive sounds of the party.

"We must pretend that we are at 221 Baker Street," Paul said. "And, here is Sherlock Holmes," a gesture to bring me forward, "with our very own Dr. Jean Watson!"

Applause.

"Welcome, sir," Jean said, turning to Paul. "And what brings you to Baker Street?"

"The loss of a very valuable necklace." He repeated the description of the bauble.

I took out my pipe and mimed a deep and satisfying inhalation of the weed. I needed a moment, to tell the truth. I love an audience and I love center stage, but there is always that dicey moment when one leaves the wings, when a deep breath is required. Especially when working without a script; especially when the future of the Sherlock Holmes Museum might require a solution as well as a delay.

"Where was the necklace kept?" Sherlock began.

"Normally at the bank, but Julia took it out for this party. It was in its case on her dressing table."

"A locked case?"

Paul shook his head. "It being normally in the safe deposit box."

"And who had access to the room besides you and your wife?"

"Agnes, the housekeeper. She's been with us thirty years. And Edith, the chambermaid; she is new but came highly recommended.

The decorator was in and out of the house all day. Various friends used the room next door to change, and Martin, the butler, has been bringing coats and wraps up to a dressing room we'd cleared."

"When did your wife last see the necklace?"

"She opened the case last night when I brought it from the bank."

"And who else would have been in the room last night?"

"Just the two of us."

"So it most likely disappeared sometime during the day today or even this evening?"

"That is likely. We never locked our rooms."

That left a more than twelve-hour window for the necklace to vanish. "I'd like to examine Mrs. Bergman's room, if I might."

The guests made to follow, but I held up my hand. "If you could wait in the foyer? Dr. Watson will be able to give you a full report of my findings." I winked at Jean but she didn't smile back.

Upstairs, the house was laid out on a traditional plan with a center hallway and a row of bedrooms opening on either side. Paul Bergman indicated the impromptu cloakroom and the rooms used by their guests to freshen their makeup or change into formal wear from their winter garb. It didn't take an expert to see that this was a terribly insecure venue for anything valuable and portable.

Julia Bergman's bedroom was toward the front of the house with a fine bay window, half blocked by another enormous wreath. She was an elegant woman with well-styled gray hair and a beautiful dove gray velvet dress. She was sitting on a *chaise longue* and from the look of her red and swollen eyes, she had just succeeded in getting her emotions under control.

"What a lovely room," Sherlock said, looking around. Besides the wreath and a green swag on the mantelpiece, smaller and daintier versions of the golden angels and reindeer disported themselves on every chest and bureau, along with a table top Christmas tree glowing with fairy lights. I took all this in, before examining the windows and the rug as the real Sherlock would have done, but nothing caught my eye. No tell-tale clay from the west of Sussex or the borders of the Thames. No special Turkish cigarette papers. No prints of a pair of boots with something wrong with one heel.

I asked her the same questions I'd asked her husband about the necklace and about who might have had access to the room without getting any further. To be honest, I was on the verge of losing both investigation and character when I smelled something in the air. The pine forest, of course. And a little perfume. Subtle, that, and doubtless pricey. And something else. Paint? Solvent? Spray paint? That was it; we'd had a little incident of vandalism via spray paint at the museum.

"I'm very taken with your beautiful decorations," I said. "Were they made on site?"

"Oh, no, St. Armond's Design brings in everything, ready to arrange."

"There must be a lot of paint used on the figures. The gold effect is really convincing."

"Styrofoam and *papier mache* underneath, though I'd never have guessed. They've been done for weeks," she said.

I had the feeling she thought me rather a fool. Just the same, I went around the room and examined every single angel and deer.

"When will your decorations be taken down?" I asked, as I touched the collar of one of the reindeer.

"The day after Christmas. At least the figurines. We have a big party planned for the New Year, and I want to tweak the *décor* for that."

Right, I thought. I always like to tweak my *décor* for the New Year. But Sherlock, better focused, had the shape of an idea. And saw an ingenious scheme.

"I'd planned to wear my necklace then," Jean said and stifled a sob. "It was my great grandmother's."

"I can assure you that you'll wear the necklace for the New Year party," I said. "Now, if you would come downstairs with me, I think we can entertain your guests and recover the necklace. Maybe catch the perpetrator, too, but I won't promise that."

"But my necklace!" She stood up in agitation.

"Quite safe. Do bear with me for a moment."

Downstairs, I asked Paul Bergman to go to his wife's room and let no one in until Dr. Watson came upstairs. The guests trooped into the living room, where Sherlock Holmes questioned Julia Bergman about the decorations in her bedroom, specifically when they had been installed.

"Everything was in two days ago."

"Absolutely everything?"

"Well, Porter—Porter St. Armond—he stops by every day to be sure the greenery is kept fresh. He brought in one more reindeer this afternoon. He said the balance of the room wasn't quite right."

"Were you in the room when this figure was delivered?"

"No. I was busy with the caterer. I told him just to take it up-stairs."

"And the reindeer was complete? I mean, all painted and with its decorations on."

"Oh, yes, as I explained to you upstairs. Everything was made and painted long ago."

"Dr. Watson, would you go up and ask Mr. Bergman to bring down the small reindeer on the table at the side window?"

Jean went upstairs looking very nervous. I felt a little guilty about keeping her in suspense, but if you can't surprise your Watson, who are you going to surprise?

"And I think, Mrs. Bergman, that we will need some nail polish remover. Would you have some?"

"There should be some in the powder room."

A thin blond woman who was clearly one of Julia's friends, stepped up. "I'll look," she said and hurried into the foyer, as Paul Bergman and My Watson came downstairs carrying the reindeer.

"Please set it on the table," Sherlock said and turned back to the assembled guests. "The decorators provided a spectacular array of figures. I noticed that there were half a dozen designs for the deer and as many for the angels, but this little fellow is different in two ways. He has a more elaborate collar for one thing. And when I was in Mrs. Bergman's room, I smelled paint, although she assured me that the figures had been prepared well in advance. This is the item that recently had been painted."

Sherlock lifted the collar from the figure and laid it on the table. Jean Bergman gave a gasp. "It's in the shape of my necklace."

"That's right." Sherlock took the nail polish that her friend had found and dabbed a little on the collar. Under the gold coating, a diamond winked. "Your necklace didn't leave your room until just a moment ago, but it would have gone out the door when the decorations were collected."

Just then the doorbell rang and a uniformed officer stepped into the foyer.

"A timely arrival," said Sherlock Holmes. "You can tell the police that your decorator has attempted to steal the LaFarge necklace."

There was a huge round of applause, and it was several minutes before the officer was recognized as a *bona fide* representative of the law and not an extra in our little drama. Paul Bergman shook my hand enthusiastically, and Julia had to be restrained from attempting to clean the necklace right then and there.

"We're so grateful," I heard her tell My Watson. "The necklace has been in the family since the Gilded Age."

"We are immensely popular," My Watson announced as I drove her home. She had needed a very stiff bourbon and ginger to settle her nerves and then another one to celebrate. "A lavish donation is to be expected. But, please, never another show like that. My nerves won't take it."

"Nonsense," I said, high from the performance and still half Sherlockian. "Your nerves, dear Watson, must be of sterner stuff. For really, it was elementary."

✗

Janice Law writes novels and non-fiction as well as short stories. Her most recent book is the Lambda mystery finalist, *Moon over Tangier* featuring the gay, alcoholic painter, Francis Bacon. It is the last volume of a trilogy published by Mysteriouspress.com.She lives with her husband, a sportswriter, in Connecticut.

SPIDERS

by Cenydd Ros

Horror gripped Detective McMather. Terror and dread. It welled up from his belly like a twisted knot of snakes and stuck in his throat, choking him. He was certain he was going to die, and it was going to happen sooner than he would have liked.

A spider ran across the ceiling. Then another... and another. It always amazed McMather how spiders could do that. He hated the little monsters. Horrible little vampires, binding their prey and sucking the life out of them. Dozens more raced across the floor, moving fast on eight legs.

"It's all in your head," McMather told himself, only half believing. "They're not real."

Then again, maybe they were. He couldn't be sure any more.

How long have I been here?

He couldn't remember. Was it three days? Was it four? It was a dangerous business working as a narc. Especially when you were a dirty narc. He tugged on the metal cuff around his wrist. Tugged on the chain securing it to the wall. Doing so made his arm ache. He glanced down. His veins were purple and swollen. His whole arm was swollen, and there was a nasty vicious red around the puncture marks where they forced the needles in.

They're going to have to cut it off.

The thought of losing his arm sent the most profound sense of sorrow and humility through him.

A man's not supposed to lose his arm. A truck, sure, a house, or his job, but not his arm.

The infection was bad. It was deep. There was no way around it. They were going to have to chop it off.

His stomach cramped and he threw himself up against the cold stone concrete wall. Was it concrete? Maybe it was just gray wallpaper. He couldn't be sure, but all the same it felt cold. His whole body was cold.

They're going to take my arm off.

It kept ringing in his mind.

Hell, I'll be dead before that.

He wished to God that his captors would hurry up and give him another needle full. Then a thought worse than death crept into his mind.

Maybe they won't be back. Maybe they're through with me and won't give me any more.

McMather began to whimper. Or was it a laugh? The sounds he made panned back and forth from despair to hysterics. Pathetic sounds. Defeated sounds. He was disgusted with himself. Disgusted at his weakness. Sickened by his need. It didn't matter, he still wanted that shot.

Spiders ran across his arms, and up his neck. He clawed at them.

"Oh, God, oh, God," he whimpered. He tried to get hold, to calm his mind. "It isn't real. It isn't real." It was no good. Holding his mind steady was like trying to balance gelatin on the edge of a knife. His body twisted in agony. A gagging spasm took him and he retched. Nothing came up. Nothing had come up for days now. Maybe a little spittle and some foam, but nothing else.

He tilted his head toward the door. That familiar scraping sound from the hall. His heart raced in anticipation. The sensation of reprieve suddenly filled him, like a man sprung from death row.

They're coming! They haven't forgotten me!

Were they coming to relieve his anguish, or were they coming to finish him off—to finally sink their fangs into his flesh and drain him of fluid? Either way, his skin would suffer another puncture.

A loud bang on the cell door. Spiders ran in all directions. The metal clank of the latch being lifted. They were coming in. The door opened. The female stepped into the room. She had the needle in her hands. She was a queen bitch of spiders. She moved toward him and he slid from the bed and whimpered beneath her.

McMather got up to his knees and begged like a dog for the potion. She kicked him with her cheap knock-off army boots.

Does she have two legs? Only two?

He thought that she did, but her hands looked like claws. Still, he drooled with anticipation and wanting what she held in them.

Sweet bliss to make the pain go away.

He knew it was venom, but he wanted it so badly.

"Please, put it in," he begged her.

"Is this what you want, little piggy?" she said, in that snide tone she always used with him. "You're beggin' for it now, oinker, just look at you." She pushed the needle in. "Not such the tough guy any more, are you?"

Warm honey sunshine flowed through his veins. McMather heaved to the floor in ecstasy. His breathing eased.

She turned and walked out of his cell, slamming the door behind her. The latch clanged down. Then silence. McMather lay on the hard ground, moaning in bliss and satisfaction. The spiders were gone.

Or are they?

He thought he could still see them, there—in the corner of his eye. Yes, they scurried still, but just out of clear view. They would come back soon enough and crawl all over him.

He got back to his knees again and began to sob.

"This has got to stop. It has to stop." He knew what he had to do. What all animals caught in a snare had to do.

They're going to chop it off, anyway.

The thought burned in his mind like a blinding truth.

McMather began to gnaw at his wrist, tearing into the flesh. It didn't really hurt. The heroin-amphetamine cocktail the whore had given him dulled the pain. That, and the week he had gone without sleep. He was beyond feeling real bodily pain. There were too many new pains to drown them out. The phantasmal pains were much worse than any real physical pains. He had been shot once, in the line of duty. That had been bad, but what his mind had manufactured in these past few days was much worse than that hot piece of lead had been.

He bit deeper into his wrist. He could do this. He must.

✗　　✗　　✗　　✗

Time floated by on a cloud of cocaine.

Jamie lay on the stained sofa. The smell of burning marijuana and cocaine filled her nostrils. Nothing smelled better to Jamie than burning cocaine. She fondled her coca-puff lovingly as she smoked it, admiring the spider tattoo on her hand. Part of the gang now, all official like.

And when you're part of something you have responsibilities. She had something to do, but she wasn't sure what it was. It was in the back of her mind, tugging at her. A task to perform. Something for Bernard. And he would be mad if she forgot to do it. That much she did remember.

Like an answer to a riddle, the bastard spoke.

"What time is it?"

He sat in front of the television watching *Gilligan's Island* in his spotted boxer shorts. Not a spotted pattern, just spotted. Brown and yellow. He had a beer in one hand and a coca-puff of his own in the other.

"It's six," she said, and coughed. Her voice was hoarse and her throat thick with mucus from the smoke.

"How long since you dosed that pig?" Bernard snarled his face in disgust. He hated cops like religion.

"Been four hours, or about," she said.

"Four hours." Bernard chuckled under a wheeze. "He's still riding the tail of it, but how about we give him another?" Bernard held the coca-puff between his lips and scratched at his groin.

Jamie cracked a smile. She thought maybe he had crabs. She hoped he did have crabs. That would serve him right. She stood up and walked toward him.

"He was on his knees begging for it last time I went in."

"Yeah, he's ripe, I think." Bernard held up a syringe. "It's time we give him his farewell ticket." His scabby lips twisted in a big grin and his yellow teeth showed. "This one is hot. He'll go out with a bang."

The thought of being the one to put the cop down made her hands shake. Jamie picked up the beer can and took a long pull off of it. Swill. Cheap crap. It was all Bernard drank, but it soothed her dry throat.

"You want me to send him over the top? How come I got to do it?"

"Don't argue with me, bitch, just O.D. the bastard," he said, and looked back to the fool on the TV. "I fixed the needle, so we're in this together. Like a family."

She coughed, chunky phlegm spilling her lip onto her chin. She wiped it away.

"Is there a problem?" Bernard's voice had a hint of danger to it. "You wanted in."

"No, no prob." She took the needle from him. "Guess this makes me a… killer, huh?"

"You're a Spider, now, Baby," he said, and then laughed at the fool on the TV.

✗   ✗   ✗   ✗

The first hour he gnawed at the flesh and muscle, chewing through the tendons and larger veins. The following hours he spent using his teeth to dislodge the small bones of his wrist. When he removed a sufficient number, he pulled hard against the steel band restraining him and his hand jerked free with a popping sound. After that, he waited. Patience.

And then the cell door opened.

McMather watched as the female came in holding the needle. He watched her from his corner, out of sight and just behind the door. She didn't react like he thought she would. She didn't panic at his apparent absence. She seemed dazed. Her eyes were fixed on the bloody mattress and his severed hand lying on the floor next to it. A blood-spray painted the wall, and a small puddle of blood had formed on the floor.

"Jesus Christ," she managed, her body trembling. "Jesus Christ. Crazy bastard ripped off his hand." But how had he gotten out of the room?

She spun around to find McMather staring at her.

"Spiders," McMather muttered.

Jamie felt a warm wet sensation between her legs. She pissed her jeans. "Oh, God."

His face was like looking into a nightmare, pale clammy flesh, mouth crusted with dried drool and bile. The end of his right forearm ended in the jagged nub of bone. Blood dripped on the floor.

"Do you see the spiders?" he asked.

"You're out of your mind, Chief. Just take it easy, okay?" Her shoulders shuddered in fear.

The madman glared at her with a fire in his eyes. Hatred.

McMather knew what to do. The thought was clear in his mind. He had been waiting for the past hour to do it. He lunged forward, jabbing his ragged exposed bone into Jamie's jugular vein. Blood rocketed from her neck and coated the wall behind him. It drenched his vomit-stained shirt.

"Got you, you damned spider!"

Jamie slumped to the floor. She dropped the needle from her hand and it bounced away. She lifted her head and gazed up at her killer in shock, her eyes bulging. McMather reached down and picked up the syringe. He jabbed it into her left eyeball and pushed the plunger down. Foam and blood boiled from Jamie's mouth. She slumped over dead.

McMather stepped into the hallway. Spiders climbed up and down the walls. He shut his eyes for a moment, squeezing them tight.

Have to keep moving forward. Keep moving or they will get you. They can't bite if you just keep moving.

McMather stepped into the kitchen. He closed his hand around the handle of a steak knife. He wasn't left handed and it felt odd in his grip.

Will have to get used to that.

In the next room, another large spider sat in his chair laughing at the TV. He gulped down beer and sucked on a coca-puff.

Bernard looked at the clock in annoyance.

"What's taking that bitch so long. I need a shot." Bernard hit the remote and flipped off the TV. He stood up and a cheap re-volver, an import Saturday-Night Special, fell off his lap and onto the floor. Bernard bent down and picked the gun up and set it on the coffee table.

He turned around just as the knife plunged into his stomach.

McMather watched the giant spider fall and curl up on the floor.

Bernard moaned, looking up at the police detective standing over him.

"You son-of-a-bitch," he hissed at McMather and pulled the knife from his belly. It slid from his hand. The cop had stabbed him good. Done a proper job of it. The pain was agonizing. He struggled to sit up. He couldn't do it. Could barely even breathe. He rolled over to his side and rested his face against the cold tile floor as the blood spilled out.

"Pig," he wheezed out.

"God-damned spiders." McMather raised his foot over Bernard's head. "I'll show you." He stomped down. Stomped down. Stomped down repeatedly on the side of Bernard's face. "I'll smash you. I'll smash all you damned spiders!"

The sound of bone crunching filled McMather's ears. He reached down and picked up the .38 caliber from the floor. He aimed and pulled the trigger. Pulled it again and again. The spider was dead at his feet.

✗　✗　✗　✗

The gunshots brought the police. An ambulance soon followed.

They strapped him into the gurney.

"You think he'll be all right?" the young officer asked his sergeant.

"Are you kidding me? He gnawed off his own hand." The sergeant shook his head. "Those bastards had him for more than a week. His mind is completely fried."

"At least he got a little payback."

"Yeah. Yeah, I guess that's something." The sergeant watched as paramedics pushed the gurney up into the ambulance. "Too bad. He was a good man. What a waste."

✗　✗　✗　✗

Inside the ambulance, McMather couldn't move. The spiders had ensnared him once again in their web. He struggled, but it was no use. The web was too strong, holding him down on his back. Thousands of the eight-legged monsters climbed over him. He wanted to scream, but he didn't have the strength. All he could do was whimper. The sound of his own pathetic sobbing made him sick. He felt defeat creep into his heart.

The paramedic looked down on him in pity and frustration.

"What the hell are they going to do with this poor bastard?"

"I don't know. He sure is a mess," the ambulance driver responded. "I'm amazed he didn't bleed to death."

"I've seen a few amputation cases," the paramedic responded. "The body has a way of taking care of itself." All he could do was to try to ease the suffering, if only a little. There was nothing else for it. One more shot wasn't going to do any damage. He injected the morphine into his patient's arm.

McMather looked up at the giant spider in the white coat glaring at him. Its four pairs of eyes sparkled down like stars. He felt the small bite on his arm, but could do nothing. He felt the venom rush through his veins, then closed his eyes and fell into the cloud.

"God-damned spiders."

THE WAY IT IS

by Carole Buggé

You lie on your bed late at night listening to the swoosh of passing cars in the rain on the street outside. There's a round, rumbling sound as they roll over the manhole cover in front of the building, a double, one-*two* percussion as the wheels pass over the metal cover, first the front and then the back wheels. It's a friendly sound, like a hollow drum, and it keeps you company as you stare at the tiny silver stars swirling around in your lava lamp. You imagine each star as a lost soul, caught up in the hot liquid of the lamp, forever circling around each other. The stars are swimming in their purple lava bath, the cars are plowing through a February thunderstorm, but you are warm and dry on your bed, covered with the quilt your mother gave you for Christmas. You lie listening to the raindrops hitting the air conditioner. You see the words the sounds spell out in your head: *plunck, plop, thrrat, rat-a-thwop plat.*

You're always happier when it's raining, especially at night when you don't have to go out and you can lie on top of your bed with your mother's quilt wrapped around your knees. It's a comfort, the rain, and you begin to imagine what would happen if it never stopped raining, if the water from the East River began to rise until it flooded its banks and everyone would have to move to higher ground.

Move to higher ground.

There is no higher in New York—downtown, where you live, is flat as a skillet. The water would just spread over everything until the city was under water. It's what happened in New Orleans, but New York has never suffered from a natural disaster like Hurricane Katrina, only man-made disasters.

What rained out of the sky that day was death, death in the form of religious fanaticism. You've had your bout with mysticism, and you're still not sure that trees don't have spirits, but you have trouble understanding the allure of organized religion.

But there it was that day, swooping down like a big, ugly bird of prey, suddenly swallowing the southern tip of the island. You've tried:

Talking it out.

Crying it out.

Swallowing it and moving on.

But what you can't stop is the image of your sister, arriving with the rest of the catering staff, so excited, so happy to be working at Windows on the World. You remember the phone call the night before:

"How are you going to fix your hair?"

"I don't know, Kelley, I haven't thought about it."

You tried not to dampen her enthusiasm, but you never had her keen spirit. You were the sensible one, the quiet one, but she was the one people looked at when she entered rooms—even though you were identical twins, it was always her shining, eager face that drew stares.

"I'm going to put mine in French braids. I think that will be elegant but it will keep it out of my face."

French braids. Her snow-blond hair, wrapped around itself in a coil like strands of DNA endlessly repeating bits of information, genetic codes that mapped out the existence of a human being, a single organism. And now these strands exist only in you—but you feel not so much like a human being as leftover matter, like the tail of a comet that has passed on into another star system.

You were supposed to be there; you had your clothes all carefully laid out the night before, but you awoke in the night with the flu, with chills and vomiting that shook your body and left you breathless and sweating. It seems like such a crummy excuse now, though, and you are left with the feeling that you should have been there. But this is the way it is: you weren't there.

Kelley was there, though, no doubt on time as usual, bouncy and bright in her starched white chef's coat. What she wanted from life was so simple: to cook for people, to make and serve them well-prepared, healthy food. What was so unreasonable about that—why, you wonder, was it too much to ask to make a life out of nourishing people? She planned to open her own restaurant someday—a small, intimate place with good prices and even better food. You would work for her—you were always more comfortable in your position as second fiddle, and she was always so gracious, so grateful to you for your devotion.

A car passes by outside, hitting a large puddle and splashing rain water onto the sidewalk. You imagine a pedestrian jumping out of the way, like a Laurel and Hardy movie. Except that Stan Laurel eventually would end up pushing Oliver

Hardy into the puddle by mistake, then, feeling bad about it, would whimper in that high-pitched whine of his until a sputtering Hardy forgave him.

Forgiveness.

Your last shrink was a Buddhist and encouraged you to forgive—forgive yourself, forgive others, and ask others for forgiveness. Good advice, except that how could you ask Kelley, when she isn't here any more? *Please forgive me for not dying with you, Kelley.*

You've tried saying it to her departed spirit, but you don't really believe in life after death, so it never feels like anyone is listening.

You glance over at the matte knife on the bedside table, its blade reflecting silver in the glow of the lava lamp like the gleaming silver planes that rained down on the city that day. In books and movies people always use razor blades, but a matte knife is so much easier to handle. You imagine sinking into the warm water in the bathtub, letting it cover your body. It will only sting for a moment, you think, and then a long slow slide into unconsciousness.

And then you will be with Kelley.

C.E. Lawrence is the author of nine published novels, award-winning plays, musicals, poetry and short fiction, some under Carole Buggé. Titan Books recently reissued her Sherlock Holmes novel, *The Star of India*. Her ebook *Silent Stalker* is the most recent of her Lee Campbell thrillers.

THE ADVENTURE OF THE COPPER BEECHES

by Sir Arthur Conan Doyle

"To the man who loves art for its own sake," remarked Sherlock Holmes, tossing aside the advertisement sheet of the *Daily Telegraph*, "it is frequently in its least important and lowliest manifestations that the keenest pleasure is to be derived. It is pleasant to me to observe, Watson, that you have so far grasped this truth that in these little records of our cases which you have been good enough to draw up, and, I am bound to say, occasionally to embellish, you have given prominence not so much to the many *causes célèbres* and sensational trials in which I have figured but rather to those incidents which may have been trivial in themselves, but which have given room for those faculties of deduction and of logical synthesis which I have made my special province."

"And yet," said I, smiling, "I cannot quite hold myself absolved from the charge of sensationalism which has been urged against my records."

"You have erred, perhaps," he observed, taking up a glowing cinder with the tongs and lighting with it the long cherry-wood pipe which was wont to replace his clay when he was in a disputatious rather than a meditative mood—"you have erred perhaps in attempting to put colour and life into each of your statements instead of confining yourself to the task of placing upon record that severe reasoning from cause to effect which is really the only notable feature about the thing."

"It seems to me that I have done you full justice in the matter," I remarked with some coldness, for I was repelled by the egotism which I had more than once observed to be a strong factor in my friend's singular character.

"No, it is not selfishness or conceit," said he, answering, as was his wont, my thoughts rather than my words. "If I claim full justice for my art, it is because it is an impersonal thing—a thing beyond myself. Crime is common. Logic is rare. Therefore it is upon the logic rather than upon the crime that you should dwell. You have degraded what should have been a course of lectures into a series of tales."

It was a cold morning of the early spring, and we sat after breakfast on either side of a cheery fire in the old room at Baker Street. A thick fog rolled down between the lines of dun-coloured houses, and the opposing windows loomed like dark, shapeless blurs through the heavy yellow wreaths. Our gas was lit and shone on the white cloth and glimmer of china and metal, for the table had not been cleared yet. Sherlock Holmes had been silent all the morning, dipping continuously into the advertisement columns of a succession of papers until at last, having apparently given up his search, he had emerged in no very sweet temper to lecture me upon my literary shortcomings.

"At the same time," he remarked after a pause, during which he had sat puffing at his long pipe and gazing down into the fire, "you can hardly be open to a charge of sensationalism, for out of these cases which you have been so kind as to interest yourself in, a fair proportion do not treat of crime, in its legal sense, at all. The small matter in which I endeavoured to help the King of Bohemia, the singular experience of Miss Mary Sutherland, the problem connected with the man with the twisted lip, and the incident of the noble bachelor, were all matters which are outside the pale of the law. But in avoiding the sensational, I fear that you may have bordered on the trivial."

"The end may have been so," I answered, "but the methods I hold to have been novel and of interest."

"Pshaw, my dear fellow, what do the public, the great unobserv- ant public, who could hardly tell a weaver by his tooth or a com- positor by his left thumb, care about the finer shades of analysis and deduction! But, indeed, if you are trivial. I cannot blame you, for the days of the great cases are past. Man, or at least criminal man, has lost all enterprise and originality. As to my own little practice, it seems to be degenerating into an agency for recovering lost lead pencils and giving advice to young ladies from boarding- schools. I think that I have touched bottom at last, however. This note I had this morning marks my zero-point, I fancy. Read it!" He tossed a crumpled letter across to me.

It was dated from Montague Place upon the preceding evening, and ran thus:

> "DEAR MR HOLMES:—I am very anxious to consult you as to whether I should or should not accept a situation which has been offered to me as governess. I shall call at half-past ten to-morrow if I do not inconvenience you. Yours faithfully,
>
> "VIOLET HUNTER."

"Do you know the young lady?" I asked.

"Not I."

"It is half-past ten now."

"Yes, and I have no doubt that is her ring."

"It may turn out to be of more interest than you think. You remember that the affair of the blue carbuncle, which appeared to be a mere whim at first, developed into a serious investigation. It may be so in this case, also."

"Well, let us hope so. But our doubts will very soon be solved, for here, unless I am much mistaken, is the person in question."

As he spoke the door opened and a young lady entered the room. She was plainly but neatly dressed, with a bright, quick face, freckled like a plover's egg, and with the brisk manner of a woman who has had her own way to make in the world.

"You will excuse my troubling you, I am sure," said she, as my companion rose to greet her, "but I have had a very strange experience, and as I have no parents or relations of any sort from whom I could ask advice, I thought that perhaps you would be kind enough to tell me what I should do."

"Pray take a seat, Miss Hunter. I shall be happy to do anything that I can to serve you."

I could see that Holmes was favourably impressed by the manner and speech of his new client. He looked her over in his searching fashion, and then composed himself, with his lids drooping and his finger-tips together, to listen to her story.

"I have been a governess for five years," said she, "in the family of Colonel Spence Munro, but two months ago the colonel received an appointment at Halifax, in Nova Scotia, and took his children over to America with him, so that I found myself without a situation. I advertised, and I answered advertisements, but without success. At last the little money which I had saved began to run short, and I was at my wit's end as to what I should do.

"There is a well-known agency for governesses in the West End called Westaway's, and there I used to call about once a week in order to see whether anything had turned up which might suit me. Westaway was the name of the founder of the business, but it is really managed by Miss Stoper. She sits in her own little office, and the ladies who are seeking employment wait in an anteroom, and are then shown in one by one, when she consults her ledgers and sees whether she has anything which would suit them.

"Well, when I called last week I was shown into the little office as usual, but I found that Miss Stoper was not alone. A prodigiously stout man with a very smiling face and a great heavy chin which rolled down in fold upon fold over his throat sat at her elbow with a pair of glasses on his nose, looking very earnestly at the ladies who entered. As I came in he gave quite a jump in his chair and turned quickly to Miss Stoper.

"'That will do,' said he; 'I could not ask for anything better. Capital! capital!' He seemed quite enthusiastic and rubbed his hands together in the most genial fashion. He was such a comfortable-looking man that it was quite a pleasure to look at him.

"'You are looking for a situation, miss?' he asked.

"'Yes, sir.'

"'As governess?'

"'Yes, sir.'

"'And what salary do you ask?'

"'I had four pounds a month in my last place with Colonel Spence Munro.'

"'Oh, tut, tut! Sweating—rank sweating!' he cried, throwing his fat hands out into the air like a man who is in a boiling passion. 'How could anyone offer so pitiful a sum to a lady with such attractions and accomplishments?'

"'My accomplishments, sir, may be less than you imagine,' said I. 'A little French, a little German, music, and drawing—'

"'Tut, tut!' he cried. 'This is all quite beside the question. The point is, have you or have you not the bearing and deportment of a lady? There it is in a nutshell. If you have not, you are not fitted for the rearing of a child who may some day play a considerable part in the history of the country. But if you have why, then, how could any gentleman ask you to condescend to accept anything under the three figures? Your salary with me, madam, would commence at 100 pounds a year.'

"You may imagine, Mr Holmes, that to me, destitute as I was, such an offer seemed almost too good to be true. The gentleman, however, seeing perhaps the look of incredulity upon my face, opened a pocket-book and took out a note.

"'It is also my custom,' said he, smiling in the most pleasant fashion until his eyes were just two little shining slits amid the white creases of his face, 'to advance to my young ladies half their salary beforehand, so that they may meet any little expenses of their journey and their wardrobe.'

"It seemed to me that I had never met so fascinating and so thoughtful a man. As I was already in debt to my tradesmen, the advance was a great convenience, and yet there was something un-natural about the whole transaction which made me wish to know a little more before I quite committed myself.

"'May I ask where you live, sir?' said I.

"'Hampshire. Charming rural place. The Copper Beeches, five miles on the far side of Winchester. It is the most lovely country, my dear young lady, and the dearest old country-house.'

"'And my duties, sir? I should be glad to know what they would be.'

"'One child—one dear little romper just six years old. Oh, if you could see him killing cockroaches with a slipper! Smack! smack! smack! Three gone before you could wink!' He leaned back in his chair and laughed his eyes into his head again.

"I was a little startled at the nature of the child's amusement, but the father's laughter made me think that perhaps he was joking.

"'My sole duties, then,' I asked, 'are to take charge of a single child?'

"'No, no, not the sole, not the sole, my dear young lady,' he cried. 'Your duty would be, as I am sure your good sense would suggest, to obey any little commands my wife might give, pro-vided always that they were such commands as a lady might with propriety obey. You see no difficulty, heh?'

"'I should be happy to make myself useful.'

"'Quite so. In dress now, for example. We are faddy people, you know—faddy but kind-hearted. If you were asked to wear any dress which we might give you, you would not object to our little whim. Heh?'

"'No,' said I, considerably astonished at his words.

"'Or to sit here, or sit there, that would not be offensive to you?'

"'Oh, no.'

"'Or to cut your hair quite short before you come to us?'

"I could hardly believe my ears. As you may observe, Mr Holmes, my hair is somewhat luxuriant, and of a rather peculiar tint of chestnut. It has been considered artistic. I could not dream of sacrificing it in this offhand fashion.

"'I am afraid that that is quite impossible,' said I. He had been watching me eagerly out of his small eyes, and I could see a shadow pass over his face as I spoke.

"'I am afraid that it is quite essential,' said he. 'It is a little fancy of my wife's, and ladies's fancies, you know, madam, ladies's fancies must be consulted. And so you won't cut your hair?'

"'No, sir, I really could not,' I answered firmly.

"'Ah, very well; then that quite settles the matter. It is a pity, because in other respects you would really have done very nicely. In that case, Miss Stoper, I had best inspect a few more of your young ladies.'

"The manageress had sat all this while busy with her papers without a word to either of us, but she glanced at me now with so much annoyance upon her face that I could not help suspecting that she had lost a handsome commission through my refusal.

"'Do you desire your name to be kept upon the books?' she asked.

"'If you please, Miss Stoper.'"

"'Well, really, it seems rather useless, since you refuse the most excellent offers in this fashion,' said she sharply. 'You can hardly expect us to exert ourselves to find another such opening for you. Good-day to you, Miss Hunter.' She struck a gong upon the table, and I was shown out by the page.

"Well, Mr Holmes, when I got back to my lodgings and found little enough in the cupboard, and two or three bills upon the table. I began to ask myself whether I had not done a very foolish thing. After all, if these people had strange fads and expected obedience on the most extraordinary matters, they were at least ready to pay for their eccentricity. Very few governesses in England are getting

100 pounds a year. Besides, what use was my hair to me? Many people are improved by wearing it short and perhaps I should be among the number. Next day I was inclined to think that I had made a mistake, and by the day after I was sure of it. I had almost overcome my pride so far as to go back to the agency and inquire whether the place was still open when I received this letter from the gentleman himself. I have it here and I will read it to you:

"'The Copper Beeches, near Winchester.

"'DEAR MISS HUNTER:—Miss Stoper has very kindly given me your address, and I write from here to ask you whether you have reconsidered your decision. My wife is very anxious that you should come, for she has been much attracted by my description of you. We are willing to give thirty pounds a quarter, or 120 pounds a year, so as to recompense you for any little inconvenience which our fads may cause you. They are not very exacting, after all. My wife is fond of a particular shade of electric blue and would like you to wear such a dress indoors in the morning. You need not, however, go to the expense of purchasing one, as we have one belonging to my dear daughter Alice (now in Philadelphia), which would, I should think, fit you very well. Then, as to sitting here or there, or amusing yourself in any manner indicated, that need cause you no inconvenience. As regards your hair, it is no doubt a pity, especially as I could not help remarking its beauty during our short interview, but I am afraid that I must remain firm upon this point, and I only hope that the increased salary may recompense you for the loss. Your duties, as far as the child is concerned, are very light. Now do try to come, and I shall meet you with the dog-cart at Winchester. Let me know your train. Yours faithfully, JEPHRO RUCASTLE.'

"That is the letter which I have just received, Mr Holmes, and my mind is made up that I will accept it. I thought, however, that before taking the final step I should like to submit the whole matter to your consideration."

"Well, Miss Hunter, if your mind is made up, that settles the question," said Holmes, smiling.

"But you would not advise me to refuse?"

"I confess that it is not the situation which I should like to see a sister of mine apply for."

"What is the meaning of it all, Mr Holmes?"

"Ah, I have no data. I cannot tell. Perhaps you have yourself formed some opinion?"

"Well, there seems to me to be only one possible solution. Mr Rucastle seemed to be a very kind, good-natured man. Is it not possible that his wife is a lunatic, that he desires to keep the matter quiet for fear she should be taken to an asylum, and that he humours her fancies in every way in order to prevent an outbreak?"

"That is a possible solution—in fact, as matters stand, it is the most probable one. But in any case it does not seem to be a nice household for a young lady."

"But the money, Mr Holmes, the money!"

"Well, yes, of course the pay is good—too good. That is what makes me uneasy. Why should they give you 120 pounds a year, when they could have their pick for forty pounds? There must be some strong reason behind."

"I thought that if I told you the circumstances you would understand afterwards if I wanted your help. I should feel so much stronger if I felt that you were at the back of me."

"Oh, you may carry that feeling away with you. I assure you that your little problem promises to be the most interesting which has come my way for some months. There is something distinctly novel about some of the features. If you should find yourself in doubt or in danger—"

"Danger! What danger do you foresee?"

Holmes shook his head gravely. "It would cease to be a danger if we could define it," said he. "But at any time, day or night, a telegram would bring me down to your help."

"That is enough." She rose briskly from her chair with the anxiety all swept from her face. "I shall go down to Hampshire quite easy in my mind now. I shall write to Mr Rucastle at once, sacrifice my poor hair to-night, and start for Winchester to-morrow." With a few grateful words to Holmes she bade us both good-night and bustled off upon her way.

"At least," said I as we heard her quick, firm steps descending the stairs, "she seems to be a young lady who is very well able to take care of herself."

"And she would need to be," said Holmes gravely. "I am much mistaken if we do not hear from her before many days are past."

It was not very long before my friend's prediction was fulfilled. A fortnight went by, during which I frequently found my thoughts turning in her direction and wondering what strange side-alley of human experience this lonely woman had strayed into. The unusual salary, the curious conditions, the light duties, all pointed to something abnormal, though whether a fad or a plot, or whether the man were a philanthropist or a villain, it was quite beyond my powers to determine. As to Holmes, I observed that he sat frequently for half an hour on end, with knitted brows and an abstracted air, but he swept the matter away with a wave of his hand when I mentioned it. "Data! data! data!" he cried impatiently. "I can't make bricks without clay." And yet he would always wind up by muttering that no sister of his should ever have accepted such a situation.

The telegram which we eventually received came late one night just as I was thinking of turning in and Holmes was settling down to one of those all-night chemical researches which he frequently indulged in, when I would leave him stooping over a retort and a test-tube at night and find him in the same position when I came down to breakfast in the morning. He opened the yellow envelope, and then, glancing at the message, threw it across to me.

"Just look up the trains in Bradshaw," said he, and turned back to his chemical studies.

The summons was a brief and urgent one.

"Please be at the Black Swan Hotel at Winchester at midday to-morrow," it said. "Do come! I am at my wit's end. HUNTER."

"Will you come with me?" asked Holmes, glancing up.

"I should wish to."

"Just look it up, then."

"There is a train at half-past nine," said I, glancing over my Bradshaw. "It is due at Winchester at 11:30."

"That will do very nicely. Then perhaps I had better postpone my analysis of the acetones, as we may need to be at our best in the morning."

By eleven o'clock the next day we were well upon our way to the old English capital. Holmes had been buried in the morning papers all the way down, but after we had passed the Hampshire border he threw them down and began to admire the scenery. It was an ideal spring day, a light blue sky, flecked with little fleecy white clouds drifting across from west to east. The sun was shining very brightly, and yet there was an exhilarating nip in the air, which set an edge to a man's energy. All over the countryside, away to the rolling hills around Aldershot, the little red and grey roofs of the farm-steadings peeped out from amid the light green of the new foliage.

"Are they not fresh and beautiful?" I cried with all the enthusiasm of a man fresh from the fogs of Baker Street.

But Holmes shook his head gravely.

"Do you know, Watson," said he, "that it is one of the curses of a mind with a turn like mine that I must look at everything with reference to my own special subject. You look at these scattered houses, and you are impressed by their beauty. I look at them, and the only thought which comes to me is a feeling of their isolation and of the impunity with which crime may be committed there."

"Good heavens!" I cried. "Who would associate crime with these dear old homesteads?"

"They always fill me with a certain horror. It is my belief, Watson, founded upon my experience, that the lowest and vilest alleys in London do not present a more dreadful record of sin than does the smiling and beautiful countryside."

"You horrify me!"

"But the reason is very obvious. The pressure of public opinion can do in the town what the law cannot accomplish. There is no lane so vile that the scream of a tortured child, or the thud of a drunkard's blow, does not beget sympathy and indignation among the neighbours, and then the whole machinery of justice is ever so close that a word of complaint can set it going, and there is but a step between the crime and the dock. But look at these lonely houses, each in its own fields, filled for the most part with poor ignorant folk who know little of the law. Think of the deeds of hellish cruelty, the hidden wickedness which may go on, year in, year out, in such places, and none the wiser. Had this lady who appeals to us for help gone to live in Winchester, I should never have had a fear for her. It is the five miles of country which makes the danger. Still, it is clear that she is not personally threatened."

"No. If she can come to Winchester to meet us she can get away."

"Quite so. She has her freedom."

"What CAN be the matter, then? Can you suggest no explanation?"

"I have devised seven separate explanations, each of which would cover the facts as far as we know them. But which of these is correct can only be determined by the fresh information which we shall no doubt find waiting for us. Well, there is the tower of the cathedral, and we shall soon learn all that Miss Hunter has to tell."

The Black Swan is an inn of repute in the High Street, at no distance from the station, and there we found the young lady waiting for us. She had engaged a sitting-room, and our lunch awaited us upon the table.

"I am so delighted that you have come," she said earnestly. "It is so very kind of you both; but indeed I do not know what I should do. Your advice will be altogether invaluable to me."

"Pray tell us what has happened to you."

"I will do so, and I must be quick, for I have promised Mr Rucastle to be back before three. I got his leave to come into town this morning, though he little knew for what purpose."

"Let us have everything in its due order." Holmes thrust his long thin legs out towards the fire and composed himself to listen.

"In the first place, I may say that I have met, on the whole, with no actual ill-treatment from Mr and Mrs Rucastle. It is only fair to them to say that. But I cannot understand them, and I am not easy in my mind about them."

"What can you not understand?"

"Their reasons for their conduct. But you shall have it all just as it occurred. When I came down, Mr Rucastle met me here and drove me in his dog-cart to the Copper Beeches. It is, as he said, beautifully situated, but it is not beautiful in itself, for it is a large square block of a house, whitewashed, but all stained and streaked with damp and bad weather. There are grounds round it, woods on three sides, and on the fourth a field which slopes down to the Southampton highroad, which curves past about a hundred yards from the front door. This ground in front belongs to the house, but the woods all round are part of Lord Southerton's preserves. A clump of copper beeches immediately in front of the hall door has given its name to the place.

"I was driven over by my employer, who was as amiable as ever, and was introduced by him that evening to his wife and the child.

There was no truth, Mr Holmes, in the conjecture which seemed to us to be probable in your rooms at Baker Street. Mrs Rucastle is not mad. I found her to be a silent, pale-faced woman, much younger than her husband, not more than thirty, I should think, while he can hardly be less than forty-five. From their conversation I have gathered that they have been married about seven years, that he was a widower, and that his only child by the first wife was the daughter who has gone to Philadelphia. Mr Rucastle told me in private that the reason why she had left them was that she had an unreasoning aversion to her stepmother. As the daughter could not have been less than twenty, I can quite imagine that her position must have been uncomfortable with her father's young wife.

"Mrs Rucastle seemed to me to be colourless in mind as well as in feature. She impressed me neither favourably nor the reverse. She was a nonentity. It was easy to see that she was passionately devoted both to her husband and to her little son. Her light grey eyes wandered continually from one to the other, noting every little want and forestalling it if possible. He was kind to her also in his bluff, boisterous fashion, and on the whole they seemed to be a happy couple. And yet she had some secret sorrow, this woman. She would often be lost in deep thought, with the saddest look upon her face. More than once I have surprised her in tears. I have thought sometimes that it was the disposition of her child which weighed upon her mind, for I have never met so utterly spoiled and so ill-natured a little creature. He is small for his age, with a head which is quite disproportionately large. His whole life appears to be spent in an alternation between savage fits of passion and gloomy intervals of sulking. Giving pain to any creature weaker than himself seems to be his one idea of amusement, and he shows quite remarkable talent in planning the capture of mice, little birds, and insects. But I would rather not talk about the creature, Mr Holmes, and, indeed, he has little to do with my story."

"I am glad of all details," remarked my friend, "whether they seem to you to be relevant or not."

"I shall try not to miss anything of importance. The one unpleasant thing about the house, which struck me at once, was the appearance and conduct of the servants. There are only two, a man and his wife. Toller, for that is his name, is a rough, uncouth man, with grizzled hair and whiskers, and a perpetual smell of drink.

Twice since I have been with them he has been quite drunk, and yet Mr Rucastle seemed to take no notice of it. His wife is a very tall and strong woman with a sour face, as silent as Mrs Rucastle and much less amiable. They are a most unpleasant couple, but fortunately I spend most of my time in the nursery and my own room, which are next to each other in one corner of the building.

"For two days after my arrival at the Copper Beeches my life was very quiet; on the third, Mrs Rucastle came down just after breakfast and whispered something to her husband.

"'Oh, yes,' said he, turning to me, 'we are very much obliged to you, Miss Hunter, for falling in with our whims so far as to cut your hair. I assure you that it has not detracted in the tiniest iota from your appearance. We shall now see how the electric-blue dress will become you. You will find it laid out upon the bed in your room, and if you would be so good as to put it on we should both be extremely obliged.'

"The dress which I found waiting for me was of a peculiar shade of blue. It was of excellent material, a sort of beige, but it bore unmistakable signs of having been worn before. It could not have been a better fit if I had been measured for it. Both Mr and Mrs Rucastle expressed a delight at the look of it, which seemed quite exaggerated in its vehemence. They were waiting for me in the drawing-room, which is a very large room, stretching along the entire front of the house, with three long windows reaching down to the floor. A chair had been placed close to the central window, with its back turned towards it. In this I was asked to sit, and then Mr Rucastle, walking up and down on the other side of the room, began to tell me a series of the funniest stories that I have ever listened to. You cannot imagine how comical he was, and I laughed until I was quite weary. Mrs Rucastle, however, who has evidently no sense of humour, never so much as smiled, but sat with her hands in her lap, and a sad, anxious look upon her face. After an hour or so, Mr Rucastle suddenly remarked that it was time to commence the duties of the day, and that I might change my dress and go to little Edward in the nursery.

"Two days later this same performance was gone through under exactly similar circumstances. Again I changed my dress, again I sat in the window, and again I laughed very heartily at the funny stories of which my employer had an immense *répertoire*, and which he told inimitably. Then he handed me a yellow-backed novel, and moving my chair a little sideways, that my own shadow might not fall upon the page, he begged me to read aloud to him. I read for about ten minutes, beginning in the heart of a chapter, and then suddenly, in the middle of a sentence, he ordered me to cease and to change my dress.

"You can easily imagine, Mr Holmes, how curious I became as to what the meaning of this extraordinary performance could possibly be. They were always very careful, I observed, to turn my face away from the window, so that I became consumed with the desire to see what was going on behind my back. At first it seemed to be impossible, but I soon devised a means. My hand-mirror had been broken, so a happy thought seized me, and I concealed a piece of the glass in my handkerchief. On the next occasion, in the midst of my laughter, I put my handkerchief up to my eyes, and was able with a little management to see all that there was behind me. I confess that I was disappointed. There was nothing. At least that was my first impression. At the second glance, however, I perceived that there was a man standing in the Southampton Road, a small bearded man in a grey suit, who seemed to be looking in my direction. The road is an important highway, and there are usually people there. This man, however, was leaning against the railings which bordered our field and was looking earnestly up. I lowered my handkerchief and glanced at Mrs Rucastle to find her eyes fixed upon me with a most searching gaze. She said nothing, but I am convinced that she had divined that I had a mirror in my hand and had seen what was behind me. She rose at once.

"'Jephro,' said she, 'there is an impertinent fellow upon the road there who stares up at Miss Hunter.'

"'No friend of yours, Miss Hunter?' he asked.

"'No, I know no one in these parts.'

"'Dear me! How very impertinent! Kindly turn round and motion to him to go away.'

"'Surely it would be better to take no notice.'

"'No, no, we should have him loitering here always. Kindly turn round and wave him away like that.'

"I did as I was told, and at the same instant Mrs Rucastle drew down the blind. That was a week ago, and from that time I have not sat again in the window, nor have I worn the blue dress, nor seen the man in the road."

"Pray continue," said Holmes. "Your narrative promises to be a most interesting one."

"You will find it rather disconnected, I fear, and there may prove to be little relation between the different incidents of which I speak. On the very first day that I was at the Copper Beeches, Mr Rucastle took me to a small outhouse which stands near the kitchen door. As we approached it I heard the sharp rattling of a chain, and the sound as of a large animal moving about.

"'Look in here!' said Mr Rucastle, showing me a slit between two planks. 'Is he not a beauty?'

"I looked through and was conscious of two glowing eyes, and of a vague figure huddled up in the darkness.

"'Don't be frightened,' said my employer, laughing at the start which I had given. 'It's only Carlo, my mastiff. I call him mine, but really old Toller, my groom, is the only man who can do anything with him. We feed him once a day, and not too much then, so that he is always as keen as mustard. Toller lets him loose every night, and God help the trespasser whom he lays his fangs upon. For goodness's sake don't you ever on any pretext set your foot over the threshold at night, for it's as much as your life is worth.'

"The warning was no idle one, for two nights later I happened to look out of my bedroom window about two o'clock in the morning. It was a beautiful moonlight night, and the lawn in front of the house was silvered over and almost as bright as day. I was standing, rapt in the peaceful beauty of the scene, when I was aware that something was moving under the shadow of the copper beeches. As it emerged into the moonshine I saw what it was. It was a giant dog, as large as a calf, tawny tinted, with hanging jowl, black muzzle, and huge projecting bones. It walked slowly across the lawn and vanished into the shadow upon the other side. That dreadful sentinel sent a chill to my heart which I do not think that any burglar could have done.

"And now I have a very strange experience to tell you. I had, as you know, cut off my hair in London, and I had placed it in a great coil at the bottom of my trunk. One evening, after the child was in bed, I began to amuse myself by examining the furniture of my room and by rearranging my own little things. There was an old chest of drawers in the room, the two upper ones empty and open, the lower one locked. I had filled the first two with my linen, and as I had still much to pack away I was naturally annoyed at not having the use of the third drawer. It struck me that it might have been fastened by a mere oversight, so I took out my bunch of keys and tried to open it. The very first key fitted to perfection, and I drew the drawer open. There was only one thing in it, but I am sure that you would never guess what it was. It was my coil of hair.

"I took it up and examined it. It was of the same peculiar tint, and the same thickness. But then the impossibility of the thing obtruded itself upon me. How could my hair have been locked in the drawer? With trembling hands I undid my trunk, turned out the contents, and drew from the bottom my own hair. I laid the two tresses together, and I assure you that they were identical. Was it not extraordinary? Puzzle as I would, I could make nothing at all of what it meant. I returned the strange hair to the drawer, and I said nothing of the matter to the Rucastles as I felt that I had put myself in the wrong by opening a drawer which they had locked.

"I am naturally observant, as you may have remarked, Mr Holmes, and I soon had a pretty good plan of the whole house in my head. There was one wing, however, which appeared not to be inhabited at all. A door which faced that which led into the quarters of the Tollers opened into this suite, but it was invariably locked. One day, however, as I ascended the stair, I met Mr Rucastle coming out through this door, his keys in his hand, and a look on his face which made him a very different person to the round, jovial man to whom I was accustomed. His cheeks were red, his brow was all crinkled with anger, and the veins stood out at his temples with passion. He locked the door and hurried past me without a word or a look.

"This aroused my curiosity, so when I went out for a walk in the grounds with my charge, I strolled round to the side from which I could see the windows of this part of the house. There were four of them in a row, three of which were simply dirty, while the fourth was shuttered up. They were evidently all deserted. As I strolled up and down, glancing at them occasionally, Mr Rucastle came out to me, looking as merry and jovial as ever.

"'Ah!' said he, 'you must not think me rude if I passed you without a word, my dear young lady. I was preoccupied with business matters.'

"I assured him that I was not offended. 'By the way,' said I, 'you seem to have quite a suite of spare rooms up there, and one of them has the shutters up.'

"He looked surprised and, as it seemed to me, a little startled at my remark.

"'Photography is one of my hobbies,' said he. 'I have made my dark room up there. But, dear me! what an observant young lady we have come upon. Who would have believed it? Who would have ever believed it?' He spoke in a jesting tone, but there was no jest in his eyes as he looked at me. I read suspicion there and annoyance, but no jest.

"Well, Mr Holmes, from the moment that I understood that there was something about that suite of rooms which I was not to know, I was all on fire to go over them. It was not mere curiosity, though I have my share of that. It was more a feeling of duty—a feeling that some good might come from my penetrating to this place. They talk of woman's instinct; perhaps it was woman's instinct which gave me that feeling. At any rate, it was there, and I was keenly on the lookout for any chance to pass the forbidden door.

"It was only yesterday that the chance came. I may tell you that, besides Mr Rucastle, both Toller and his wife find something to do in these deserted rooms, and I once saw him carrying a large black linen bag with him through the door. Recently he has been drinking hard, and yesterday evening he was very drunk; and when I came upstairs there was the key in the door. I have no doubt at all that he had left it there. Mr and Mrs Rucastle were both downstairs, and the child was with them, so that I had an admirable opportunity. I turned the key gently in the lock, opened the door, and slipped through.

"There was a little passage in front of me, unpapered and uncarpeted, which turned at a right angle at the farther end. Round this corner were three doors in a line, the first and third of which were open. They each led into an empty room, dusty and cheerless, with two windows in the one and one in the other, so thick with dirt that the evening light glimmered dimly through them. The centre door was closed, and across the outside of it had been fastened one of the broad bars of an iron bed, padlocked at one end to a ring in the wall, and fastened at the other with stout cord. The door itself was locked as well, and the key was not there. This barricaded door corresponded clearly with the shuttered window outside, and yet I could see by the glimmer from beneath it that the room was not in darkness. Evidently there was a skylight which let in light from above. As I stood in the passage gazing at the sinister door and wondering what secret it might veil, I suddenly heard the sound of steps within the room and saw a shadow pass backward and forward against the little slit of dim light which shone out from under the door. A mad, unreasoning terror rose up in me at the sight, Mr Holmes. My overstrung nerves failed me suddenly, and I turned and ran—ran as though some dreadful hand were behind me clutching at the skirt of my dress. I rushed down the passage, through the door, and straight into the arms of Mr Rucastle, who was waiting outside.

"'So,' said he, smiling, 'it was you, then. I thought that it must be when I saw the door open.'

"'Oh, I am so frightened!' I panted.

"'My dear young lady! my dear young lady!'—you cannot think how caressing and soothing his manner was—'and what has frightened you, my dear young lady?'

"But his voice was just a little too coaxing. He overdid it. I was keenly on my guard against him.

"'I was foolish enough to go into the empty wing,' I answered. 'But it is so lonely and eerie in this dim light that I was frightened and ran out again. Oh, it is so dreadfully still in there!'

"'Only that?' said he, looking at me keenly.

"'Why, what did you think?' I asked.

"'Why do you think that I lock this door?'

"'I am sure that I do not know.'

"'It is to keep people out who have no business there. Do you see?' He was still smiling in the most amiable manner.

"'I am sure if I had known—'

"'Well, then, you know now. And if you ever put your foot over that threshold again'—here in an instant the smile hardened into a grin of rage, and he glared down at me with the face of a demon—'I'll throw you to the mastiff.'

"I was so terrified that I do not know what I did. I suppose that I must have rushed past him into my room. I remember nothing until I found myself lying on my bed trembling all over. Then I thought of you, Mr Holmes. I could not live there longer without some advice. I was frightened of the house, of the man, of the woman, of the servants, even of the child. They were all horrible to me. If I could only bring you down all would be well. Of course I might have fled from the house, but my curiosity was almost as strong as my fears. My mind was soon made up. I would send you a wire. I put on my hat and cloak, went down to the office, which is about half a mile from the house, and then returned, feeling very much easier. A horrible doubt came into my mind as I approached the door lest the dog might be loose, but I remembered that Toller had drunk himself into a state of insensibility that evening, and I knew that he was the only one in the household who had any influence with the savage creature, or who would venture to set him free. I slipped in in safety and lay awake half the night in my joy at the thought of seeing you. I had no difficulty in getting leave to come into Winchester this morning, but I must be back before three o'clock, for Mr and Mrs Rucastle are going on a visit, and will be away all the evening, so that I must look after the child. Now I have told you all my adventures, Mr Holmes, and I should be very glad if you could tell me what it all means, and, above all, what I should do."

Holmes and I had listened spellbound to this extraordinary story. My friend rose now and paced up and down the room, his hands in his pockets, and an expression of the most profound gravity upon his face.

"Is Toller still drunk?" he asked.

"Yes. I heard his wife tell Mrs Rucastle that she could do nothing with him."

"That is well. And the Rucastles go out to-night?"

"Yes."

"Is there a cellar with a good strong lock?"

"Yes, the wine-cellar."

"You seem to me to have acted all through this matter like a very brave and sensible girl, Miss Hunter. Do you think that you could perform one more feat? I should not ask it of you if I did not think you a quite exceptional woman."

"I will try. What is it?"

"We shall be at the Copper Beeches by seven o'clock, my friend and I. The Rucastles will be gone by that time, and Toller will, we hope, be incapable. There only remains Mrs Toller, who might give the alarm. If you could send her into the cellar on some errand, and then turn the key upon her, you would facilitate matters immensely."

"I will do it."

"Excellent! We shall then look thoroughly into the affair. Of course there is only one feasible explanation. You have been brought there to personate someone, and the real person is imprisoned in this chamber. That is obvious. As to who this prisoner is, I have no doubt that it is the daughter, Miss Alice Rucastle, if I remember right, who was said to have gone to America. You were chosen, doubtless, as resembling her in height, figure, and the colour of your hair. Hers had been cut off, very possibly in some illness through which she has passed, and so, of course, yours had to be sacrificed also. By a curious chance you came upon her tresses. The man in the road was undoubtedly some friend of hers—possibly her fiancé—and no doubt, as you wore the girl's dress and were so like her, he was convinced from your laughter, whenever he saw you, and afterwards from your gesture, that Miss Rucastle was perfectly happy, and that she no longer desired his attentions. The dog is let loose at night to prevent him from endeavouring to communicate with her. So much is fairly clear. The most serious point in the case is the disposition of the child."

"What on earth has that to do with it?" I ejaculated.

"My dear Watson, you as a medical man are continually gaining light as to the tendencies of a child by the study of the parents. Don't you see that the converse is equally valid. I have frequently gained my first real insight into the character of parents by studying their children. This child's disposition is abnormally cruel, merely for cruelty's sake, and whether he derives this from his smiling father, as I should suspect, or from his mother, it bodes evil for the poor girl who is in their power."

"I am sure that you are right, Mr Holmes," cried our client. "A thousand things come back to me which make me certain that you have hit it. Oh, let us lose not an instant in bringing help to this poor creature."

"We must be circumspect, for we are dealing with a very cunning man. We can do nothing until seven o'clock. At that hour we shall be with you, and it will not be long before we solve the mystery."

We were as good as our word, for it was just seven when we reached the Copper Beeches, having put up our trap at a wayside public-house. The group of trees, with their dark leaves shining like burnished metal in the light of the setting sun, were sufficient to mark the house even had Miss Hunter not been standing smiling on the door-step.

"Have you managed it?" asked Holmes.

A loud thudding noise came from somewhere downstairs. "That is Mrs Toller in the cellar," said she. "Her husband lies snoring on the kitchen rug. Here are his keys, which are the duplicates of Mr Rucastle's."

"You have done well indeed!" cried Holmes with enthusiasm. "Now lead the way, and we shall soon see the end of this black business."

We passed up the stair, unlocked the door, followed on down a passage, and found ourselves in front of the barricade which Miss Hunter had described. Holmes cut the cord and removed the transverse bar. Then he tried the various keys in the lock, but without success. No sound came from within, and at the silence Holmes's face clouded over.

"I trust that we are not too late," said he. "I think, Miss Hunter, that we had better go in without you. Now, Watson, put your shoulder to it, and we shall see whether we cannot make our way in."

It was an old rickety door and gave at once before our united strength. Together we rushed into the room. It was empty. There was no furniture save a little pallet bed, a small table, and a basketful of linen. The skylight above was open, and the prisoner gone.

"There has been some villainy here," said Holmes; "this beauty has guessed Miss Hunter's intentions and has carried his victim off."

"But how?"

"Through the skylight. We shall soon see how he managed it." He swung himself up onto the roof. "Ah, yes," he cried, "here's the end of a long light ladder against the eaves. That is how he did it."

"But it is impossible," said Miss Hunter; "the ladder was not there when the Rucastles went away."

"He has come back and done it. I tell you that he is a clever and dangerous man. I should not be very much surprised if this were he whose step I hear now upon the stair. I think, Watson, that it would be as well for you to have your pistol ready."

The words were hardly out of his mouth before a man appeared at the door of the room, a very fat and burly man, with a heavy stick in his hand. Miss Hunter screamed and shrunk against the wall at the sight of him, but Sherlock Holmes sprang forward and confronted him.

"You villain!" said he, "where's your daughter?"

The fat man cast his eyes round, and then up at the open skylight.

"It is for me to ask you that," he shrieked, "you thieves! Spies and thieves! I have caught you, have I? You are in my power. I'll serve you!" He turned and clattered down the stairs as hard as he could go.

"He's gone for the dog!" cried Miss Hunter.

"I have my revolver," said I.

"Better close the front door," cried Holmes, and we all rushed down the stairs together. We had hardly reached the hall when we heard the baying of a hound, and then a scream of agony, with a horrible worrying sound which it was dreadful to listen to. An elderly man with a red face and shaking limbs came staggering out at a side door.

"My God!" he cried. "Someone has loosed the dog. It's not been fed for two days. Quick, quick, or it'll be too late!"

Holmes and I rushed out and round the angle of the house, with Toller hurrying behind us. There was the huge famished brute, its black muzzle buried in Rucastle's throat, while he writhed and screamed upon the ground. Running up, I blew its brains out, and it fell over with its keen white teeth still meeting in the great creases of his neck.

With much labour we separated them and carried him, living but horribly mangled, into the house. We laid him upon the drawing-room sofa, and having dispatched the sobered Toller to bear the news to his wife, I did what I could to relieve his pain. We were all assembled round him when the door opened, and a tall, gaunt woman entered the room.

"Mrs Toller!" cried Miss Hunter.

"Yes, miss. Mr Rucastle let me out when he came back before he went up to you. Ah, miss, it is a pity you didn't let me know what you were planning, for I would have told you that your pains were wasted."

"Ha!" said Holmes, looking keenly at her. "It is clear that Mrs Toller knows more about this matter than anyone else."

"Yes, sir, I do, and I am ready enough to tell what I know."

"Then, pray, sit down, and let us hear it, for there are several points on which I must confess that I am still in the dark."

"I will soon make it clear to you," said she; "and I'd have done so before now if I could ha' got out from the cellar. If there's police-court business over this, you'll remember that I was the one that stood your friend, and that I was Miss Alice's friend, too.

"She was never happy at home, Miss Alice wasn't, from the time that her father married again. She was slighted like and had no say in anything, but it never really became bad for her until after she met Mr Fowler at a friend's house. As well as I could learn, Miss Alice had rights of her own by will, but she was so quiet and patient, she was, that she never said a word about them but just left everything in Mr Rucastle's hands. He knew he was safe with her; but when there was a chance of a husband coming forward, who would ask for all that the law would give him, then her father thought it time to put a stop on it. He wanted her to sign a paper, so that whether she married or not, he could use her money. When she wouldn't do it, he kept on worrying her until she got brain-fever, and for six weeks was at death's door. Then she got better at last, all worn to a shadow, and with her beautiful hair cut off; but that didn't make no change in her young man, and he stuck to her as true as man could be."

"Ah," said Holmes, "I think that what you have been good enough to tell us makes the matter fairly clear, and that I can deduce all that remains. Mr Rucastle then, I presume, took to this system of imprisonment?"

"Yes, sir."

"And brought Miss Hunter down from London in order to get rid of the disagreeable persistence of Mr Fowler."

"That was it, sir."

"But Mr Fowler being a persevering man, as a good seaman should be, blockaded the house, and having met you succeeded by certain arguments, metallic or otherwise, in convincing you that your interests were the same as his."

"Mr Fowler was a very kind-spoken, free-handed gentleman," said Mrs Toller serenely.

"And in this way he managed that your good man should have no want of drink, and that a ladder should be ready at the moment when your master had gone out."

"You have it, sir, just as it happened."

"I am sure we owe you an apology, Mrs Toller," said Holmes, "for you have certainly cleared up everything which puzzled us. And here comes the country surgeon and Mrs Rucastle, so I think, Watson, that we had best escort Miss Hunter back to Winchester, as it seems to me that our *locus standi* now is rather a questionable one."

And thus was solved the mystery of the sinister house with the copper beeches in front of the door. Mr Rucastle survived, but was always a broken man, kept alive solely through the care of his devoted wife. They still live with their old servants, who probably know so much of Rucastle's past life that he finds it difficult to part from them. Mr Fowler and Miss Rucastle were married, by special license, in Southampton the day after their flight, and he is now the holder of a government appointment in the island of Mauritius. As to Miss Violet Hunter, my friend Holmes, rather to my disappointment, manifested no further interest in her when once she had ceased to be the centre of one of his problems, and she is now the head of a private school at Walsall, where I believe that she has met with considerable success.

www.ingramcontent.com/pod-product-compliance
Lightning Source LLC
Chambersburg PA
CBHW051850170626
46807CB00003B/1411